"Are you insecure about the way you look?" he asked lazily, and if Caitlin could have gone any redder, she would have.

"Of course not!" She whipped her head away and stared out at the marvelous vista, not really seeing any of it but instead conjuring up an unflattering picture of herself alongside Luisa. She thought of all those leggy beauties next to whom she knew she often came up short in the eyes of the opposite sex. Tears gathered in the corners of her eyes and she took a deep breath, refusing to give in to the weak temptation to feel sorry for herself.

"Because you shouldn't be." The words left Dante's mouth, a silky murmur that was as dangerous as a dark incoming tide. "The likes of Luisa Sofia Moore can't hold a candle to you."

He raked his fingers through his hair. He'd broken eye contact but he was still alive to her warmth, the feel of her next to him.

"It's not just about how you look," he breathed, reluctantly turning back to her, ensnared by the pure crystal green of her eyes. "So why is he with you? That's what I find so puzzling. Nobody has ever talked to me the way you have. So, you and my brother, Alejandro, who has never been known to say boo to a goose? No. I'm just not getting it."

Caitlin didn't say anything and, into the silence, Dante continued roughly.

"Me," he breathed, "I'm the sort of man who could handle you. Not my brother."

Cathy Williams can remember reading Harlequin books as a teenager, and now that she is writing them, she remains an avid fan. For her, there is nothing like creating romantic stories and engaging plots, and each and every book is a new adventure. Cathy lives in London, and her three daughters—Charlotte, Olivia and Emma—have always been, and continue to be, the greatest inspirations in her life.

Visit the Author Profile page at Harlequin.com for more titles.

Cathy Williams

THE FORBIDDEN
CABRERA BROTHER

HARLEQUIN®
PRESENTS®

Recycling programs
for this product may
not exist in your area.

ISBN-13: 978-1-335-14888-9

The Forbidden Cabrera Brother

Copyright © 2020 by Cathy Williams

This edition published by arrangement with Harlequin Books S.A.

For questions and comments about the quality of this book,
please contact us at CustomerService@Harlequin.com.

Harlequin Enterprises ULC
22 Adelaide St. West, 40th Floor
Toronto, Ontario M5H 4E3, Canada
www.Harlequin.com

Printed in U.S.A.

THE FORBIDDEN
CABRERA BROTHER

CHAPTER ONE

SOMETHING, DANTE THOUGHT as he nursed his whisky and stared out at the floodlit manicured gardens that comprised the grounds of his Spanish estate, wasn't making sense.

Behind him he could hear the muffled sound of voices and laughter—all those people, from dignitaries to old family friends, who had gathered to welcome Alejandro, his older brother by four years, and his fiancée.

It was a star-studded event, even though it had been arranged at fairly short notice. Such was the long arm of the Cabrera family's influence that an invitation from them—especially, Dante recognised, one that would be hosted at his own sprawling mansion—pretty much guaranteed attendance.

Intricate lanterns twinkled up the long winding private avenue that led to his house. Behind him, on a warm summer night, the bank of French doors at the back of his house had been flung open wide to a vision of exactly what extreme wealth could get. The serving staff on high alert for empty glasses, the blaze of yet more lanterns adorning the strategically placed trees and illuminating the still splendour of his infinity pool, the massive ice sculpture of a couple, which his mother had insisted on having. And, of course, the very elegant, barely noticeable and extremely expensive trio of violinists providing subtle background music. Here, in this setting, the women in their high-designer elegance and the men, formally dressed, were birds of paradise at home in a setting with which they were largely familiar.

His parents, naturally, were bristling with excitement at meeting a woman who, as far as they were concerned, was roughly five years overdue. Tradition was tradition and, as the eldest in the family and now in his mid-thirties, Alejandro should have been duly wed and well on the way to producing an heir or two to the throne.

The vast fortunes tied up with the Cabrera name needed to be kept in the family and Roberto and Isabella Cabrera had been making noises about grandchildren for some time now. How else could the family lineage remain intact if both their sons decided that playing the field was a far better option than settling down to the rigours of domestic life?

Dante was as keen as his parents were for Alejandro to get married and have kids because if he didn't, then it wouldn't be long before their parents began looking to Dante to do his duty in that area and he most certainly wasn't up for that.

So when Alejandro had phoned three weeks ago

with the happy tidings that he was engaged, it had been champagne all round, a suitably lavish engagement party hastily arranged and expectations running high.

One small snag, though, was the fiancée.

Where the hell was she?

Shouldn't the loving couple have arrived together? Holding hands and staring into each other's eyes with undisguised adoration? It wasn't as though they had been dating for years and had had time to settle into the comfortable routine of taking one another for granted. Oh, no, the fiancée had been produced like a white rabbit from a magician's hat, so young love should still be fresh enough for the woman to have accompanied Alejandro to the opulent engagement party happening inside.

Except, she hadn't and—Dante glanced at his watch before swallowing the remainder of the whisky—it was a mere two hours before the elaborate buffet was set out and the speeches began. Half an acre of lawn had been meticulously roped off so that tables could be laid out with no small detail spared, from the linen cloths to the magnificent arrangements of red roses, as befitting a couple in love. The seating was casual because it was a party, and yet it still managed to feel incredibly formal in its opulence.

He wondered whether the mysterious bride-to-be would deign to make an appearance in time or whether his brother would have to mumble his apologies while the guests tucked into finest prepared rib of roast suckling pig in the absence of his fiancée. Certainly, Alejandro was strangely phlegmatic about the woman's appalling lack of manners. Maybe he had become a little too accustomed to the behaviour of a high-maintenance woman who felt that drama was some kind of selling point. Dante wryly thought that he had encountered a few of those himself.

He was about to turn away and head back into the sitting room, where champagne and canapés would be in full flow, when something caught his eye. In the twilight gloom, he glimpsed movement up the winding tree-lined private avenue that led to the courtyard in front of the house.

Standing still, he squinted and there it was again, a movement barely glimpsed between the trees.

He dumped his glass on the broad concrete ledge, straightened up and headed down the sweeping arc of stone steps that descended gracefully towards the open courtyard and then out towards the drive.

Caitlin could barely see. Up ahead, the lawns and a mansion of unseemly proportions were illuminated by the sort of floodlit extravaganza that could be seen from space. Here, as she half ran up the tree-lined avenue leading to the house, the path dipped in and out of the shadows. Any minute now and her already nightmarish trip would be compounded by an even more nightmarish ending, which would involve her tripping over something, breaking her ankle and having to be carried ignominiously into the house on a makeshift stretcher.

Everything had gone wrong, starting with her mother sobbing down the end of the phone just as she was supposed to be leaving for the airport, and ending with the taxi, booked by Alejandro to fetch her from the airport and deliver her to her own engagement party, for heaven's sake, getting a flat tyre just when she didn't need it.

Now, three hours late, she'd decided that creeping into the house and at least having the option of getting ready somewhere private was far the more sensible choice, rather than the screech of a taxi alerting everyone to her lateness.

She shuddered at the thought of all those assembled guests piling out of the front door to witness her dishevelled appearance. In his understated way, Alejandro had warned her that it was going to be *something of a bash*—which, in Alejandro-speak, meant that there would be ten thousand people there, all waiting for her arrival.

As luck would have it, Alejandro was, as always, nowhere near his mobile phone and her quiet entry through a side door somewhere was disappearing with each reluctant step forward. She'd tried calling him a dozen times and every single time it had gone to voicemail and she was fed up of leaving increasingly despairing messages.

They were supposed to be in love! In the real

world, he would be hanging on the end of the line, worried sick about where she was!

Caitlin thought of him and couldn't help but smile because that was just Alejandro. He would have dumped his phone on a random table somewhere and would have to be reminded that she still hadn't arrived, which was something of a big deal because the engagement party his parents had arranged had been for both of them.

Not for the first time, she felt a twinge of intense discomfort at this story they had concocted. Back in London, it had seemed almost inevitable because it had satisfied so many disparate concerns, but here...

She stopped in her tracks to catch her breath and gazed at the mansion towering ahead of her, ablaze with lights. The courtyard was massive, as big as a football field, and it was crammed with high-end cars of every description. They were parked at haphazard angles but, when she squinted, she could make out two men in uniform and she guessed that they would be in charge of parking so that any of the luxury cars could be moved at the snap of a finger. She shivered with apprehension.

This was reality now. They weren't in London any longer. They weren't sharing their sob stories over a bottle of wine. A plan had been made and she had temporarily turned a blind eye to the fact that plans made in one country appeared completely different when viewed in another.

Posing as Alejandro's fiancée had been the answer

to both their problems and, in London, that solution had seemed a logical conclusion.

But here…

With the sounds of summer insects around her and the grandeur of a sprawling house reminding her that this was where a simple game was always going to lead…

Her heart raced and she half looked over her shoulder with an instinctive urge to run away.

About to speed-dial Alejandro for the umpteenth time, she was only aware of a man stepping out of the shadows when he was practically on top of her and she didn't stop to think before taking action. It had been drummed into her by her parents the minute she decided to leave Ireland for the streets of London that it didn't pay to trust anyone. London, they had intoned worriedly, was a dangerous place. Accordingly, Caitlin had learned the basics of self-defence and now those ten lessons at the local town hall once a week coalesced into a blood-curdling shriek as she swung her holdall at the looming figure, striking a direct hit against his shoulder.

She had been aiming for his head, but the man was tall, way taller than her five foot three. She snapped her hands into action and eyed him narrowly for a few seconds as she debated which manoeuvre to take.

If only she were taller! Leaner! Stronger! Instead, she was short, round and it was dawning on her at speed that she probably wasn't going to land any significant punches because this stranger was built like a house.

She grasped her holdall tightly and took the next most sensible option, which was flight.

She didn't get far. One minute, she was half running and panting with her eyes pinned to the mansion in the distance. The next minute, a vice-like grip was holding her back, at which point she spun round and kicked.

'What the...?' Dante demanded, holding her at arm's length as she struggled and tried to sling punches at him.

'Get *off* me!'

'Stop trying to kick me!'

'Stop trying to attack *me*! You have no idea who you're dealing with! I... I'm an expert in martial arts!'

Dante released her. He was temporarily stunned into silence. He couldn't quite make her out because it was dark, but he could see enough to realise that the pint-sized spitfire rubbing her arm was about as expert in martial arts as he was in ballet dancing.

'I don't know who you are,' Caitlin gritted, backing away just in case he decided to lunge at her, 'but if you don't clear off, I'm going to make sure that the police are contacted as soon as I get to...' she nodded brusquely at the house, which should have been a lot closer considering how far she'd walked but still seemed a hundred miles away '...that house you can see up there.'

'You're going up there? Why?'

'That's none of your business.' She spun round and began walking as fast as she could towards her destination. If the guy lurking in the grounds was up to no good, then he had obviously realised that she didn't make a good candidate to be robbed. One glance at her dress code would have given the game away. Long flowered skirt, sensible shoes, her favourite flowing blouse over which, because it was cool even though it was summer, she was prudently wearing a cardigan...not a diamond in sight.

She clasped her holdall ever tighter, because you never knew... She didn't want to look at him, even though her skin tingled because he had fallen into step alongside her. She had no intention of making eye contact.

'It might be.' Dante had always had the knack of making people stop dead in their tracks without raising his voice and, on cue, she stopped.

'What are you talking about?'

'Engagement party? Alejandro? Name ring bells?' He folded his arms and stood perfectly, watchfully still.

Caitlin turned to the stranger. They had progressed out of the shadowy overhang of trees, into more light, and she could make him out far more clearly and suddenly her mouth went dry and her nervous system seemed to temporarily forget what it was meant to do.

He had stepped back and she saw he was dressed

for—yes, an engagement party. Black trousers, white shirt with the top couple of buttons undone as though he couldn't be bothered with a formal dress code, no tie. He'd shoved his hands in his pockets, dragging down the trousers ever so slightly, and that seemed to emphasise the perfection of his muscular frame.

Her breathing went from fast to slow and back to fast in record time. She blinked, confused at a reaction that was so out of keeping with the person she knew herself to be.

When she met his eyes, she had to try to ignore the impact of a perfectly chiselled face. The man oozed sex appeal. He was also ever so slightly familiar, but she knew that she would remember him if she'd ever met him, or even laid eyes on him. He was not a man anyone could meet and forget.

'You're here for the engagement party, as well.' She finally found her voice and then, because she was irritated with herself for being thrown by him, she belatedly added, 'In which case why are you lurking in the grounds and jumping out at perfect strangers?'

She began walking, once more, in the direction of the house. Time was of the essence at this point and she couldn't waste any more of it chatting to someone who made the hairs on the back of her neck stand on end.

But this time her awareness of him, once again falling into step alongside her, was acute. She could feel the rasp of her breathing, and the shadow he cast as the winding tree-lined avenue became ever more brightly lit sent shivers racing up and down her spine.

Only when she was standing to the side, with the massive edifice of the house in front of her, did she stop to take stock, at which point she tried Alejandro's number once again. She felt sick and out of her depth. She'd always known that Alejandro came from a wealthy background, but to be thrust into the very vortex of it, as she was now, made her stomach clench.

The cars that filled the vast courtyard gleamed with the patina of priceless machinery. Up close, the house, brightly lit, was beyond impressive and the distant thrum of noise was a sick reminder that the part she had undertaken to play was not going to be an easy one.

Predictably, Alejandro failed to respond.

'Problems?'

'Why are you still here?' Her voice was laced with agitation.

'I thought I'd personally escort you to the premises,' Dante said.

'Don't you believe that I'm a legitimate guest?'

At that, Dante inspected her with leisurely thoroughness, his dark eyes roving from the tips of her toes, along her body and finally coming to rest on her scarlet face.

She had gone into attack mode from the second he had surprised her and she was still in it. If she was a guest, then she was a highly unlikely guest.

'Are you? Because you don't seem to be dressed for the part.'

At that, Caitlin reddened even more. Her parents had always made a point of telling her that she was beautiful, inside and out, but parents were notoriously partisan and she had always been sensitive about her looks. She'd stopped longing to be five inches taller and fifteen pounds lighter, a leggy brunette free from the curse of freckles and hair the most skilled hairdresser would have found impossible to tame, but right now...

With this impossibly sexy and perfect guy lounging in front of her and staring with just the hint of a condescending smile on his face...

'I have clothes in here,' she said coldly, indicating her holdall with a curt nod. 'And in case you're in any doubt that I actually *have* been invited to this engagement party, I should tell you that I happen to be the...er... Alejandro's fiancée.' It wasn't a declaration that rolled easily off the tongue. Downright lies seldom did.

Dante said nothing. He was too stunned to speak.

'I'm running a bit late...ah...anyway...'

'Alejandro's fiancée?' He found his voice. He was seldom thrown, but this time he was.

'There's no need to sound so incredulous.' There was, actually, every need. Not even she, with her imagination going full pelt, found it easy to believe that she could possibly be Alejandro's fiancée. They came from such different worlds. Whatever his back story and however close they had become over time, he was Spanish nobility and it was there in the way he held himself and his casual disregard for money. He could do as he pleased, even if he was funny and caring and considerate, which always left you with the illusion that he couldn't buy the world, which he could. Somehow, you always expected the super rich to run roughshod over people and Alejandro completely disproved that theory. That, of course, was one of the reasons why she absolutely adored him.

They were also so different to look at. She was pale, with freckles and green eyes and copper-coloured hair. He was swarthy and dark-haired. They were both short, though, and plump and she felt wonderfully comfortable with him.

'Miss Walsh?'

'Caitlin. Look, I can't hang around here chatting to you. I have to…' She squinted at the imposing edifice of the house and tried to work out a possible side entrance through which she could sneak, although heaven only knew what she would do if and when she did enter the house if Alejandro was still missing in action. Fumble her way to the downstairs loo so that she could change into her finery? Hope that she didn't trip over anyone in the process?

So poorly conceived all of this, a plan born on the spur of the moment without much thought being given to the technical detail. It was just as well that once this engagement party was over and done with, they would both return to London where life would carry on as normal.

She pulled her long, tumbling hair over her shoulder and fiddled with it while she tried to work out various house-entry options.

'You were saying…' Dante prompted.

Caitlin looked at Dante and shivered again. The guy had the strangest effect on her. Since when had she ever gone for the brooding Alpha-male type? She'd learned long ago to steer clear of those sorts.

Besides, men this good-looking were always far too fond of themselves for her liking. And as a postscript, she belatedly thought, she was engaged. Or at least, for all intents and purposes she was engaged. Which amounted to the same thing.

'As you mentioned,' she conceded, 'I'm not exactly dressed the part and I can't get hold of Alejandro. He's terrible when it comes to his mobile phone. It never seems to be on him.'

'I'm surprised he isn't scouring the four corners in search of his errant bride-to-be,' Dante murmured.

'What do you mean?'

'Shouldn't he be out looking for you? If you haven't been able to get hold of him to warn him of your late arrival?'

'Oh, right. Yes. I see where you're going with that,' Caitlin mumbled. 'He… We are quite relaxed with one another when it comes to stuff like that.'

'What a novel approach to a serious relationship.'

'I need to change into my glad rags.' Something

about the man's tone of voice triggered a wave of unfocused apprehension in her. 'And you never introduced yourself. You are…?'

She paused and stilled him with her hand. Her eyes met his questioningly.

For a couple of seconds, Dante's cool, rational mind seemed to shut down, then he drew back and returned her wide-eyed gaze narrowly.

'Do you know the layout of the house?' He smoothly changed the conversation, while at the same time politely removing her hand and hustling her between the cars and past the uniformed valets standing to attention outside.

Was this his brother's fiancée? Dante couldn't quite believe it, but then how was he to know what sort of woman his brother liked? He had never met any of Alejandro's girlfriends. Different countries, awkward schedules, fleeting meetings over snatched drinks in random bars. He and his brother had long mastered the art of saying absolutely nothing of any genuine importance to one another.

That said, Dante had always assumed that his brother would go for the same kind of women he did, refined thoroughbreds who moved in the same social circles as they did. When Dante thought about those women, he felt a certain amount of boredom, but the one thing he knew about them, and it was very important, was the fact that they were all independently wealthy. Largely they came from families who, if not in the same category as his, were in a similar ballpark. No gold-diggers and, from bitter experience, he knew that gold-diggers were a breed best avoided.

A memory pushed its way to the surface. He'd lost his heart once, at the tender age of nineteen, to a woman ten years older who had played him so well that he had ended up handing over wads of cash to her. A small fortune. He'd fallen for a tale of a broken marriage and a violent ex and a vulnerable toddler. She had been poor but still touchingly hopeful in the face of personal tragedies, desperate for a new start yet tentative about accepting anything from him, which had made him insist on giving her even more, and of course so breathtakingly beautiful that common sense had been quickly abandoned to a raging libido hooked on the thrill of the unknown. It had been wildly exciting after his tame diet of beautiful, predictable young socialites and privately educated heiresses. When he reflected on what might have been had he not caught her in bed with the father of her child, no less, he was filled with shame at his own stupidity, but every mistake taught a valuable lesson and he had never again strayed from what he knew. Rich, beautiful, well bred. Known territory. If they were self-absorbed and sometimes shallow, then that was a price he was willing to pay.

Caitlin Walsh was not known territory…and while *he* might have the nous to know how to handle any woman who wasn't known territory, did his brother?

A broken heart, Dante figured, was no bad thing.

It made you stronger. But his brother was engaged, and once rings had been exchanged a broken heart wouldn't be the only thing to deal with. The family fortune had to be protected and Dante had no intention of letting that out of his sight.

If Alejandro was taken in by Caitlin Walsh, then Dante saw no reason why he couldn't do a bit of probing of his own, for no other reason than to make sure Alejandro wasn't about to make the biggest mistake of his life.

Wasn't that what brotherly love was all about?

'I've never been to the house before,' Caitlin responded tartly, 'so it would be impossible for me to know the layout. I had hoped that Alejandro...'

'It's his engagement party. He's probably busy entertaining the troops. You're in luck, though. I happen to know the place very well. You might say that I know it like the back of my hand.'

Caitlin stopped and stared at him with undisguised relief. 'Would you mind...? I need to change and I would rather not...' She made a vague gesture to encompass her state of dress. 'I should have got here ages ago...but with one thing and another... If you know the house, I would really appreciate it if you could maybe...'

'Sneak you in so that you can change into your finery?' Dante stood back and looked at her from the towering height of his six feet two inches. The hold-all was quite small for finery. 'Why would I do that when I've been accused of attacking you?'

'You surprised me. Naturally I reacted accordingly.' Caitlin's voice was stiff.

'You could have caused me permanent damage,' Dante inserted smoothly, 'what with you being an expert in martial arts.' Silence greeted this remark. He could see that she was itching to launch a few verbal missiles. His antennae were still on red alert, but the woman was in a league of her own, and what had promised to be something of a tedious social occasion was looking up. When you were someone who could always call the shots, a little bit of *different* went a long way. He was beginning to enjoy this little bit of different...

'Fortunately,' he carried on magnanimously, 'I am not a man to bear a grudge and I would be delighted to secrete you away somewhere private where you can freshen up.'

'I don't know how to thank you,' Caitlin said, in a voice that was far from oozing gratitude.

Dante said nothing but, just for a second, something weird and strong raced through him, heating his blood and tightening his groin. He spun round on his heels and began heading towards the side of the house, away from the brightly lit entrance.

'You'll have to be quick,' he said, slowing briefly so that she could catch up with him. 'The party's in full swing. The longer you take, the more dramatic the reception is going to be.' He glanced at her. The braid was not quite enough to keep her fiery hair in order and wisps floated around her cheeks. She was flushed and breathing fast. His eyes dropped to breasts that were more than a handful. Small-statured and large-breasted.

Infuriated by the sudden lapse of self-control, he stiffened. If the woman was up to no good then he intended to find out before the situation became financially messy, but she was engaged to his brother and he wasn't going to forget that. Forbidden thoughts would be culled before they could start interfering with what had to be done, and in very little time because if she had angled for a profitable engagement then she wasn't going to hang around waiting for the wedding ring to seal the deal.

He took her to one of the many spare bedrooms. Each and every one was permanently prepared to a high state of readiness although it was rare for guests to stay overnight. Dante loathed that sort of thing and, indeed, the only time the vast mansion saw an influx of people was when he happened to be away and it was lent out to friends or family members. He valued his privacy far too much.

'Make yourself at home,' he drawled as she stood still and looked all around her. 'I'll wait outside for you. You won't know how to find your way down to where the action is.'

As she was busy appreciating a level of luxury she had never seen in her life before, it was a few seconds before Caitlin responded, then she eyed her holdall.

'I'm sure I'll manage,' she said dubiously.

'I'll wait.'

'Why?'

Dante felt a twinge of guilt. He needed to get a feel for her, work out if his suspicions were well founded, and time wasn't going to be on his side. His intentions could not exactly be called noble and something fleeting in her eyes, an expression of helpless, vulnerable apprehension, made him flush darkly.

'Call it good manners,' he said brusquely.

'Okay.' She hesitated, then smiled tentatively. 'I might need a bit of moral support. I'm not accustomed to…events like this… When Alejandro and I…' She reddened.

'When you and Alejandro…?'

'I knew there was going to be a party,' she said hurriedly, 'but I had no idea that it would be on this scale.'

'Alejandro comes from an extremely high-ranking family,' Dante murmured, his keen eyes taking in everything, missing nothing. 'With more notice, it would have been even bigger. As it stands, two hundred is reasonably well contained.'

'I… The cars parked outside…' She sighed. 'I'm not sure I've brought the right clothes…'

Dante thought of the women milling around downstairs, dressed to kill and dripping in diamonds. He noted her anxious expression and reminded himself that the most efficient gold-digger would always be the one least obvious. His lips thinned because he knew that better than most.

'I'm sure you'll…fit in just fine…'

'You haven't seen my outfit.' Caitlin grinned and met his veiled gaze with a roll of her eyes. 'Once you have, feel free to change your mind. I just didn't think…'

'You just didn't think…?'

'That it would be quite like this, like I said,' she told him honestly. 'I never thought that the place would be so…lavish.'

'Yet you knew that your fiancé came from a wealthy family…'

'Yes, of course, but… It doesn't matter. I'm here now so there's not much I can do about… What you can't change you might as well accept, and I definitely can't change the outfit I brought over with me. Anyway… I'm going to get ready so if you don't mind? I won't be long.'

He gave it forty minutes at the very least. Longer if something had to be done about her hair. She was so unexpected and novel an entity that he literally couldn't imagine what the transformation would be like and it annoyed him that he couldn't resist letting his imagination break its leash and run away. He responded to that by lounging against the wall, flipping open his phone and scrolling through work emails.

He was settling in for the long haul when the bedroom door was pulled open and out she breezed, all of a fluster.

He pushed himself from the wall and slowly moved to stand directly in front of her.

'That was quick.'

She looked…amazing. Gone was the fashion-disaster outfit she had been wearing. In its place was a figure-hugging jade-green dress that lovingly emphasised each and every delectable curve of her small but insanely feminine body.

The sight of it made Dante stiffen as he acknowledged, once again, just how inappropriate his reaction was.

'I forgot the diamonds at home.' There was a nervous edge to her voice and she fiddled with the thin gold chain around her neck, a sixteenth birthday present from her parents.

'I doubt anyone will notice the oversight,' Dante murmured. She was playing with a thin necklace round her neck and his dark eyes zeroed in on her slender fingers and then on the shadowy cleft between her breasts. He gritted his teeth and quickly looked away.

'It's kind of you to say so.' She fell into step with him, taking it slowly because the heels were stupidly high and falling was a distinct possibility.

'I doubt anyone has ever called me *kind*. How did you and Alejandro meet?' Dante realised that he had asked very few basic questions about the relationship that had materialised out of thin air. 'We were all…a little surprised by the speed of the relationship…'

Dante barely noticed the endless miles of corridor along which they were walking, although he was keenly aware of her wide-eyed awe. Telling but hardly surprising if there was an agenda to the fifteen-second relationship, he thought wryly. To one side, ornate wrought-iron railings offered a view of acres of marble on the ground floor and white walls on which were hung huge statement pieces of abstract art. An enormous crystal chandelier, as delicate as a waterfall, dominated the vaulted ceiling, dropping five metres down to the central hallway, which was manned by several uniformed men and which they had successfully avoided.

'We go back a way,' Caitlin said vaguely.

'He's never mentioned having a serious girlfriend in the past.'

'We were…er…friends…before…' Slanted green eyes collided with dark, coolly thoughtful ones. 'You still haven't told me who you are. I guess you must know Alejandro and his brother really well considering you're so familiar with this house. It's pretty amazing, isn't it?'

'Admittedly,' Dante murmured, completely ignoring her question, 'he hasn't let on much about anyone there in London.'

The noise was increasing in volume and then they exited into the massive hall manned by the uniformed guards, who half bowed but were clearly trained to remain in the background. The paintings here were more traditional, less abstract and more impressionistic.

Caitlin was drawn like a magnet towards one of them and inspected it minutely, lost for a few moments in the exquisite mix of colours and recognising the somewhat obscure artist behind it. It was the artwork of a connoisseur.

'It's a lovely piece.' She turned to Dante, her eyes gleaming with appreciation.

'You know about art?' Dante raised both eyebrows questioningly.

'Why shouldn't I?' Caitlin stood back. 'I'm a photographer but I studied art at college. I probably know a lot more than Alejandro's brother, even though he owns this house. I'll bet he hasn't got a clue who this artist is.'

'Why would you say that?' Dante asked silkily.

'He's a businessman,' she said with a shrug. 'I gather making money is his number one priority. I'd say that if that's the case, then he's probably commissioned someone to bulk-buy a fortune's worth of valuable artwork that will do its job and appreciate over the years and make him yet more money.'

'That's quite a statement,' Dante murmured. 'You must have gleaned that impression from somewhere… Is that what his brother has told you?'

'Of course not!' She cleared her throat. 'Alejandro never has a judgemental word to say about anyone. Not that I'm being judgemental…just expressing an opinion…'

'But surely you would be partisan, considering you're his besotted better half?' Dante was outraged that a woman who had catapulted herself into the centre of their family, for reasons that were open to a lot of question, should dare insult him in his own house. Actually, should dare insult him, full stop.

'Sorry?' Caitlin blinked then blushed. 'Yes. No. I mean, *yes*, of *course* that's what I am, but no, I'm not at all partisan. I don't know why I'm telling you all this. I still don't even know who you are!'

'Oh, haven't I introduced myself?' He gave a mocking half-bow and then fixed her with his amazing eyes. 'My oversight. I am Dante Cabrera, Alejandro's brother.'

CHAPTER TWO

'Why didn't you pick up your phone?' was the first thing Caitlin demanded when she had finally managed to corner Alejandro, who had already been tipsy by the time she'd located him.

When she and Alejandro had discussed this charade, and it had been a discussion that had not happened on the spur of the moment or even overnight, she had not foreseen the very real stumbling blocks she might encounter.

She knew that she only had herself to blame. An optimist by nature, someone who had been brought up to see the silver lining behind every cloud, she had spent months lost in the unfamiliar world of uncertainty and hopelessness. Misfortune had rained down on her from the very moment she'd found out about her parents' horrendous financial problems, and from that point on things had only seemed to get worse. Her parents had always been her biggest fans and the very backbone of her life, there for her through thick and thin, always in her corner. They had instilled positivity in her and a belief that things could only get better whenever she'd been a little low. She'd relied on them, and to see her father tearful and broken...to have faced the repercussions as they had unravelled over the past few months...

She had had to step up to the plate in a way she had never had to before. She had had to go into care-taker mode. It had been debilitating, especially as she had been working in London and commuting as often as she could back to Ireland, spending money she could ill afford because every penny she earned now had to be earmarked for the gaping hole the financial catastrophe had left in her parents' lives.

Alejandro's suggestion had, at first, fallen on bar-ren ground. The thought of any deliberate deception had been anathema to Caitlin. Every moral code in-stilled from birth had risen up against the thought of lying, but he had persisted. He had his very press-ing reasons, in many ways as urgent as hers, and he had persuaded her that she would be doing him a favour, that in return he, with his limitless millions, would be honoured to return that favour. As a friend, he had insisted, it would be an insult to him for her to turn him away in her moment of desperate need. If friends couldn't help one another when help was most needed, then what was the point?

He had said all the right things at the very time when she had been absolutely dazed at the speed with which disaster after disaster had been battering her naturally upbeat nature.

From the minute she had accepted Alejandro's

offer, a weight had been lifted and the sun had ten-tatively begun to peek out from behind the bank of raging dark clouds.

She had been able to see a way forward. The sil-ver lining had been slowly restored and that, she re-alised now, had been her undoing, because she had contrived to overlook the fact that what had started as a straightforward solution might throw up unex-pected obstacles.

She hadn't banked on the brother.

She'd been apprehensive about meeting his par-ents but nowhere in that scenario had she given a second thought to Dante, even though there had been sufficient mention of him over the time she had known Alejandro to have joined the dots and worked out that he was ruthless. With a light at the end of the tunnel, she had allowed her optimism to take over and that had been a mistake.

When Dante had disclosed his identity, her brain had done a rapid overview of the conversation they had had from the moment she had attacked him on the walk up to the house and she had realised that she would have to be careful around him.

He had laid bait for her to take and if she didn't watch out, he would…do *what*? Caitlin didn't know, because what on earth could the man do in the space of twenty-four hours, after which she would be gone? But that didn't prevent a shiver of apprehension from feathering along her spine at the nebulous thought that she should be on her guard.

She determined to avoid him for the remainder of the party, which, as she glanced now at her watch, still had a long way to go. And where on earth was her wandering fiancé? He had become close friends with the champagne and, between trying to keep an eye on him and also on Dante, she had had a hellish hour and a half.

His charming parents had almost been welcome relief. They were over the moon that their eldest was finally settling down. She had been so distracted by the tug of war inside her at having to avoid Dante, while watching out for an increasingly inebriated Alejandro, that she had only paid scant attention to their polite but searching questions about what she did and whether she would continue doing what she did once she was married. She had tried to appear focused as she had listened to their gentle but insistent hints about the grandchildren they hoped would be forthcoming sooner rather than later while her brain had conjured up alarming scenarios of what a suspicious Dante might do should he decide to make mischief. Or worse.

She had barely had the chance to feel awkward even though she knew, on some level, that she really didn't belong with this glamorous, pampered crowd. So many of them, swarming in confident groups. So many beautiful women and expensive men, barely glancing at the waiting staff as they did the rounds with champagne and canapés. To the right, there was the glorious sight of tables laid out for outdoor

. dining. It should have looked casual and homely but it looked, instead, madly opulent. There was something strangely intimidating about tables formally dressed under the stars, manned by formally attired waiting staff, like a Michelin-starred restaurant in a five-star hotel, suddenly exposed to the elements.

She would have been a lot less nervous had she not been agonisingly conscious of Dante, a tall, brooding presence, glimpsed just enough for her to know that he was keeping an eye on her.

And it wasn't just the fact that he was an unknown threat that made her jumpy…

She also remembered the way her body had reacted to him, nerves all over the place and pulses racing a mile a minute. She hadn't known who he was and her response had been instinctive and physical and shocking.

Things felt as though they were getting beyond her control. She'd barely managed to exchange two words with Alejandro, just sufficient to scramble through what had happened en route to the big event.

Now, as everyone made their way through a huge archway of flowers and lanterns into the magical outdoor eating area, Caitlin felt that she had to vent some of her panic and frustration on her so-called erstwhile fiancé, before he tipped over the edge from too much champagne.

Thanks to his absent-mindedness when it came to his phone, and his preoccupation with hurrying along the occasion by drinking as much and as fast as he could, she had ended up in a place she had not banked on and she just wasn't equipped to deal with it. Subterfuge wasn't in her genetic code and she was terrified of blurting something out to Dante, who struck her as the sort who wouldn't release the bone once he had got it between his pearly white teeth. Which he had.

His watchful, speculative dark eyes brought to mind a shark in search of prey.

When she looked at Alejandro she realised that he was miserable, and she prayed that she was the only one to spot his unhappiness underneath the broad smiles and perspiring bonhomie.

Alejandro was not being Alejandro and he was clearly a lot more uncomfortable with the situation than she was. She cornered him.

'This is a nightmare.' Alejandro was busy relieving the waiter of another flute of champagne as he leant into her. 'And I'm sorry about the phone, Linny. No idea where I left it. Still haven't found it. It's probably buried under a cushion somewhere. There was a lot of sitting around earlier today. Talking. God, this is a nightmare. And I can't believe your bad luck running into Dante on your way to the house.'

'Slow down on the drinking!' was Caitlin's anxious response to that.

'I can't. It's the only thing that's propping me up.'

'Oh, Alex.' She sighed and rubbed his arm sympathetically. 'You need to be honest with your family.'

'I will. Just not yet. Once Dante finds a woman

and settles down, then the pressure will be off me and then…' His voice drifted off. It was a conversation they had had before. 'Are you going to be all right?'

'What do you mean?'

'People can sit where they please but close friends and family members are at the top table. Wedding style. Look at where you're sitting.' He'd been propelling her along on unsteady legs and now he nodded to the one and only table with a seating plan. It occupied an exalted position on a makeshift podium that was adorned with striking flowers in urns of various sizes.

'Why have they stuck me next to your brother?' Caitlin was appalled and panic bloomed inside her. She had optimistically thought that she might have seen off Dante for the remainder of the evening. She had planned on vanishing with Alejandro at a respectable hour, when the guests started drifting off. A flight had been booked. He had assured her that his parents wouldn't bat an eye because they were used to work commitment cutting short all kinds of family gatherings, usually courtesy of Dante.

Still reeling from the prospect of sitting next to Dante, she raised her eyes to spot him heading in her direction. His gait was leisurely, his body language was relaxed but he was a man on a mission. She shivered. The shark looked in the mood for a meal and she quailed at the thought of being the tasty morsel. She was barely aware of Alejandro. She was too busy telling herself that the evening would be over soon enough.

'I suppose,' she surfaced to hear Alejandro muttering gloomily, 'the intention is for you to get to know the nearest and dearest. Don't worry, Uncle Alfredo to your right is okay and Dante has Luisa next to him on the other side.'

'Luisa?' She was riveted at the sight of Dante weaving his way through the crowd, so graceful, so dangerously, darkly beautiful. He was compelling. She felt a little sick and wished all over again that she had stuck to her guns but, when she thought about her parents and the mess they were in, she could see why she had done what she had.

'Not here yet. She enjoys making an entrance. My hopes are high for Dante and Luisa to do what everyone expects they'll eventually do.'

'What's that?' she asked vaguely.

'Tie the knot. They dated a year or so ago and broke up but everyone thinks it's just a matter of time before it all kicks off again. Anyway, I have to go, Caitlin. You'll have my moral support from across the table. Feel for me. As the guest of honour, I will have both parents on either side so it's going to be an evening of the Spanish Inquisition. I just can't cope.'

'You'll have to,' Caitlin said sternly.

There was a bewildering array of wine glasses in front of them and she only hoped that his nerves wouldn't propel him to have them all filled so that he could duly empty them. He wasn't a drinker. Frankly, she was surprised that he was still standing.

When she shifted her attention away from him, it was to find that Dante was settling into the chair next to her and she shivered and began a hurried conversation in broken Spanish with Uncle Alfredo, as he wanted to be called, who was very happy to carry the conversation.

The night air was balmy and the sky was velvet black, dotted with stars. It was a perfect setting and were this a real engagement party, it would have been heavenly. She thought back to that distant time when it had looked as though marriage might have been hers for the taking and felt a rush of sadness. It had ended and it had been for the best, but sitting here, in this wonderful, magical setting, she could almost airbrush away the expensively dressed people and imagine what it might be like to be celebrating a true engagement to a guy she loved, under the stars, with the gentle sound of violins harmonising with the chirping of invisible summer insects.

'We meet again…'

Caitlin blinked and landed back on Planet Earth with a resentful bump. 'You should have told me who you were,' she said stiffly, bypassing small talk, which seemed irrelevant now, considering they were already acquainted.

'Is that why you've spent the evening avoiding me? Because you were embarrassed?'

'I wasn't avoiding you.' While there was a buffet service for the guests, this select table benefited from an array of assiduous waiters whose duty was to make sure they were fed and watered without having to exert themselves at all.

It was over-the-top luxury that Caitlin could have done without. No opportunity to take her time hovering in front of tables groaning with food. No opportunity to duck Dante's dark, fascinating, menacing presence.

There wasn't even Luisa there to distract. Whoever she was. Caitlin had paid scant attention at the time, but there was an empty chair next to him so the woman was obviously going to be a no-show.

'I, naturally, would have told you who I was but you gifted me a unique opportunity to get to know the real you. The real Caitlin Walsh, mystery fiancée.'

'There's nothing mysterious about me.' Her heart was racing and her mouth was dry.

'Which, in itself, is something of an enigma. I've watched your interaction with Alejandro and, yes, I can see that you two are close. He seeks you out with his eyes when you're not around.'

'Like I said,' Caitlin said, sotto voce, picking at an arrangement of appetisers on a plate that had found its way in front of her and pointedly making sure not to look at Dante, 'we've been friends for ages.'

'Yes, the friend bit,' Dante intoned smoothly, his low murmur matching hers, 'is evident. It's the other bit I'm not seeing.'

'I have no idea what you're talking about.'

'Where's the touchy-feely, loved-up, starry-eyed, can't-stand-a-metre-apart-from-one-another couple?' His voice oozed concerned curiosity and Caitlin gritted her teeth together and wished he would just disappear.

'We're not those people.' She shifted back as a waiter bowed to remove her plate. There seemed to be an army of them, moving as one, making sure that everything went to plan. 'We don't believe in public displays of affection. Not everyone does.' Refusing to be threatened, Caitlin peered past him to the empty seat on his left. 'And speaking of which, where's the guest who's supposed to be sitting next to you? Luisa, I believe? That's what Alejandro told me. He said that you two are practically engaged?'

Dante's lips thinned and he turned so that he was looking directly at her. 'Is that so?' he said in a sibilant murmur that would have served as a warning shot to anyone else.

'Yes…' Caitlin tilted her head to one side, considering his rhetorical question as though it were deserving of an answer '…but, of course, he may have got it all wrong. He said something about you two being an item in the past and everyone assuming that it's going to end in marriage even though you're on a break?' She couldn't help herself. She'd never thought that she could take pleasure in watching someone squirm, but for the first time since their paths had crossed Dante wasn't calling the shots and she liked it.

'This conversation is going nowhere,' he growled, under his breath.

'Lots of people go on breaks,' Caitlin murmured wickedly. 'Sometimes, taking a step back from someone can make you realise how important they are in your life. We don't know one another at all, so I hope you'll forgive me for saying what's on my mind.' She didn't give him time to do any such thing. The last thing she intended to do was stop saying what was on her mind. 'Marriage and tying the knot can be scary. Are you scared, Dante? I would say that you should let go of all those apprehensions and show Luisa how much you really care about her.' She wondered what this mystery woman was like. Beautiful, captivating…she would have to be if she'd managed to get to a guy like Dante Cabrera.

'I don't believe I'm hearing this. No one—*no one*—has ever dared address me in this way!'

'In that case, please accept my apologies,' Caitlin said without a hint of apology in her voice. 'But you feel free to ask me whatever you want to so why shouldn't I return the favour?' Their eyes collided and she felt such a rush of weird *sensation* race through her body, like the surge of an electric charge, that she blinked in utter confusion and for a few seconds couldn't say anything at all.

Then the moment was lost because there was a sudden lull in the din of people talking and all heads, as one, swung round to the arch where a leggy brunette was poised theatrically, her beautiful face a picture of exaggerated remorse. The glow of the lanterns and the backdrop of light from the house did her a lot of favours. She was aiming for drama and she was delivering it in bucketloads. Her lips twitched with amusement, inviting everyone at the honoured top table to get in on the joke with her. Caitlin could only admire the spectacle.

Then Luisa was stalking towards them, tossing her hair as a waiter scurried to hold out a chair, then it was all about Dante.

Caitlin thought she might be gaping. Up close, the woman was even more stunning than she had appeared at a distance. Perfect features in a perfectly oval face. Her hair was waist length, curling down a narrow back and, although she was olive toned—just a shade lighter than the guy sitting next to her—she had the most incredible bright blue eyes.

Caitlin politely turned away as more food continued to arrive, but she could hear breathless murmurs coming from the woman in question and not much from Dante.

Caitlin's head was whirling. She suddenly felt self-conscious. A little ridiculous in her newly acquired fancy dress and her silly high heels, pretending to be someone she wasn't.

She was back to feeling like that girl who had been ditched by the boy everyone in the village had assumed she'd end up with. Ditched for a five-foot-ten beauty from Latvia. All the insecurities Caitlin had felt then assaulted her now in a full-frontal attack, a reminder that this silly party wasn't real, that there was no engagement, that love and marriage were not things on the cards for her, and no amount of optimism and silver linings could camouflage that fact. This charade was a pragmatic solution to a problem that had been tearing her apart.

She wasn't a beauty queen like Luisa. She was the girl next door and she was ashamed of those taboo stirrings she had felt with Dante, that slow uncurling of something sexual that had blindsided her. Had she completely lost her mind? Had two glasses of champagne gone to her head?

She surfaced to find that the business of eating was beginning in earnest. The alcohol was flowing. The courses were coming thick and fast, each one a testament to what a talented chef could produce.

'I never remembered Alejandro drinking quite so much,' a deep, velvety voice to her left murmured.

Caitlin had glazed over at Alfredo's long-winded monologue about a game of golf he had played three weeks previously. She snapped to attention in a hurry at the sound of Dante's deep, dulcet tone.

She looked narrowly at Alejandro, who was flushed, before turning sideways to Dante.

'He…he…'

Dante's dark eyebrows winged upwards in a question.

'He's thoroughly enjoying his own engagement party?' Dante queried helpfully before she could think of something to say. 'If I didn't know better,

I'd almost think that he was a man trying to drown his sorrows.'

'Thankfully—' Caitlin stabbed a piece of succulent chicken breast '—you don't know better.' Her skin tingled. Something about his voice, his accent, barely there and stupidly sexy.

'Mind you,' Dante mused thoughtfully, 'he's stuck between our parents. They will be asking him all sorts of probing questions he probably doesn't know how to answer.'

'Such as what?'

'Oh, the usual. Timelines…venues…food preferences for the wedding meal…'

Caitlin remained silent. Yes, she'd been plied with a couple of those questions herself but poor Alejandro would be squirming like a fish on a hook, trying to fend off *probing questions*.

'Poor Alejandro,' Caitlin murmured softly, without thought. Too late, she realised that that was the last thing she should have said because those questioning eyebrows now conveyed less mild curiosity and more scorching interest.

'That's an odd response. Why do you say that?'

'Because…'

'Because…?' Dante prompted silkily. 'I'm all ears.'

He had moved closer to her so that his shoulder was almost but not quite brushing hers and she could smell the warmth of his breath and whatever woody cologne he was wearing. Out of the corner of her eye, she could see that Luisa had turned the full, glowing wattage of her undivided attention to the elderly man sitting next to her. There was lots of noise, people talking, laughing, getting merrier by the second as the alcohol continued to flow, served by the army of solicitous waiters. The lanterns swayed in the breeze, picking up the glitter of expensive jewellery, adding a layer of mystery to the wildly glamorous gathering.

Amidst all this, the low murmur of his voice in her ear somehow seemed to wrap them in a bubble of their own.

'We haven't talked about…er…concrete plans for anything.' She tentatively tested the waters to see whether this evasive response would have the desired effect of shutting him up. The dress was beginning to feel uncomfortable, or maybe it only felt uncomfortable because she was beginning to perspire with a sense of rising panic.

Across the table, Alejandro was not helping matters. He was tugging at his collar and guzzling champagne as though his life depended on it. She would have to corner him, somehow, and steer him back on the straight and narrow, but she had no idea how she was going to do that because there was still a long way to go with the wonderful never-ending meal and then, presumably, speeches.

'I confess I'm surprised.'

'Why?'

'I always thought that once rings were on fingers, the first thing a woman wanted to do was pin her man down to a time and a place.'

'Has that been your experience?'

'I've never been engaged. I'm surmising.'

'I guess you and Luisa…must have discussed things of that nature?'

'It won't work.'

'What won't work?'

'Trying to get me off-piste with this conversation. Don't you want to set up house as soon as you can? Alejandro is no longer a boy in his twenties. I'm sure he's keen to set the date so that he can start producing heirs to the throne.'

Caitlin contained a shudder of horror.

'It may not have occurred to you,' Caitlin said stiffly, 'that in this day and age a woman might actually want to further her career before she starts having a family. I'm only twenty-five.'

'No, if I'm being honest.'

'No *what*?'

'No, it hasn't occurred to me.'

'I love what I do.' She slanted her eyes sideways and instantly looked away because the lazy intensity in his gaze unsettled her. 'I left Ireland to make my way in London and I managed to land a very enjoyable job freelancing at a magazine. Every day is different and I have a lot of opportunities to go somewhere with my career. I may not want to sacrifice all of that to have kids when I'm still young.'

'Photographer for a magazine…' He let that musing statement hang tantalisingly in the air between them for a few seconds. 'Very interesting. Tell me, how did you and my brother meet? There's quite a chasm between the world of business and the world of entertainment and I'm racking my brains but I'm pretty sure publication isn't part of the family holdings.'

Caitlin had a moment of sheer panic. What, exactly, had Alejandro told everyone? She had been vague when questioned but the man sitting next to her wasn't going to let her get away with vague.

'No one spends all their time working,' she said faintly. 'Everyone has hobbies and Alejandro discovered that he enjoyed photography. It's…relaxing…'

'A straight answer, Caitlin. Is that asking too much? How did you meet?'

'He dropped by.' She took a deep breath. 'I happened to be renting space in a workshop. I still do, as it happens. He dropped by and we got chatting.'

'Why would he drop by a workshop?'

'You should ask him.'

'But you're sitting next to me,' he responded smoothly, 'and so I'm asking *you*.'

'He dropped by—' Caitlin glanced across to Alejandro, who was now looking the worse for wear '—and we just happened to click.'

'But you didn't start going out with one another. That happened later…'

'That's right.'

'Why is that? Was it not love at first sight? Maybe he was involved with someone else at the time? Or maybe you were?'

His low voice was a persistent murmur in her ear.

'Why are you asking all these questions?' she breathed. 'I get it that you're curious about our relationship, but, honestly, isn't it enough that I'm here? Your parents haven't pried into our...our relationship...'

'My parents are already in love with the idea that their eldest son is going to be tying the knot. They have grandchildren on their mind. They see what they want to see, but my vision is slightly less rose-tinted. Alejandro might be older than me but he's gullible in places I'm not. Gullible enough to fall hook, line and sinker in love with a woman who might not be...let's just say, right for him. So my curiosity? Natural. Your reticence on the subject of love and marriage, not to mention your reluctance to go into detail? Less natural.'

She was thinking hard. Thinking about how to address those suspicions. Loathing the man for putting her on the back foot, for not accepting what she had to say, for not being satisfied with polite small talk.

She was still thinking, still sweating with discomfort when it happened.

The crash was deafening. For a few seconds, she just couldn't seem to focus on what exactly had happened because everything seemed to have slowed down. Then she realised, in a flash, that Alejandro had fallen. He had begun standing up, but he'd had so much to drink that his legs had refused to co-operate. He'd fallen, dropped backwards like a stone, catapulting the chair behind him and crashing to the ground.

She sprang to her feet. Everyone had sprung to their feet. Then it was all a blur. She raced over to where Alejandro lay sprawled in an unnatural position on the ground, with one arm flung behind his head and his leg twisted underneath him. He was perfectly still and as she shoved her way to his side Caitlin desperately wondered whether he was breathing at all. Tears had sprung to her eyes and she was whimpering when someone pulled her back.

She felt the hardness of muscle against her back and then Dante was whispering urgently into her ear.

'Don't panic. He's alive and there's a doctor here. Take it easy.'

The voice that had filled her with discomfort and hostility only moments earlier now soothed her, but she barely had time to question the phenomenon because amidst the chaos someone was pushing forward and taking charge, ordering people to stand back while simultaneously reaching for his phone and jabbing at it as he bent towards Alejandro.

Caitlin couldn't bear to watch. She spun round and buried her head against Dante. He could have been anyone. She just couldn't look at her friend lying there on the ground. There was a roaring in her ears, which she wanted desperately to block out.

She wasn't quite sure what happened next. She knew that people were being ushered inside. So was she. Her feet were moving, propelling her towards a sitting room where she was settled on a sofa, a quiet place which was good, left on her own, time to gather herself. What had just happened replayed in her head in slow motion.

It was dark in the sitting room, with only one of the lamps on a side table on, but that suited her. Her thoughts were going crazy in her head and just when she was about to go out because she couldn't sit on her own any longer, the door was pushed open and she saw Dante outlined, a shadowy silhouette filling the frame.

'You need to sit down, Caitlin.' His voice was low and serious as he moved towards her.

She fell back against the sofa, too scared to say a word. He'd moved from the shadows into the pool of light from the lamp and his expression was as serious as his voice.

'What's happened, Dante?' she whispered.

'Sit and I'll tell you. Good news and bad…'

CHAPTER THREE

SHE WAS SHAKING like a leaf and she barely noticed the glass of brandy Dante had brought in with him. He'd been thinking ahead, she dimly registered, predicting her reaction and knowing that she would need a stiff swig of something to deal with whatever he had to say.

If the gravity of his expression wasn't enough, the very fact that he had come equipped with brandy said it all.

He'd sat her down on the sofa and he sat next to her and waited until she had fortified herself by duly sipping some of the fiery alcohol, even though she didn't feel she needed it.

'Just tell me,' she whispered.

'There was a doctor there. An eminent surgeon, as it happens. A relative on my father's side. Of course, he couldn't do a complete test but it would seem that Alejandro fell at an awkward angle. If I could draw a parallel, it's a bit like someone collapsing to the ground because the chair they'd planned on sitting on has been yanked out from under them.'

'An awkward angle…'

'He didn't fall far, but what's certain is that he's broken several small but significant bones in his ankle.'

Caitlin looked at him and blinked. Her thoughts were lagging behind but a few broken bones didn't seem like the end of the world and she said as much, breathing a sigh of relief and closing her eyes.

'Not so fast,' Dante said, and he held her gaze when she opened her eyes to stare at him.

A person could drown in those eyes, she thought distractedly. She hadn't noticed how deep and dark they were before, because she'd been arguing with him, resentful and defensive at his suspicions, which had made her question all over again the wisdom of embarking on the charade. They weren't arguing now, and something shifted and filtered through her defences. Now, as their eyes locked, she could see that his were the deepest shade of bitter chocolate and fringed with thick, sooty lashes that any woman would give her right arm for.

He was a good-looking guy and she was up close and in a state of shock. It was understandable that those first impressions, that whisper of sexual attraction, felt stronger now. 'You said he just broke a few bones…'

'Preliminary findings show that he struck his head on the marble flooring at an awkward angle. He's concussed at the moment and we won't know more until more detailed examinations are made at the hospital, but Roberto seems to think that Alejandro could slide into a temporary coma.'

'A *coma*?' Tears gathered. 'But he just had a little fall…'

'It's not a certainty so there's no need to start getting upset.'

'Of course I'm going to be upset! I should be there with him.' She stood up while Dante remained seated, his long legs stretched out and lightly crossed at the ankles.

Why wasn't he responding? How could he look so cool and collected at a time like this?

'I need to get to that hospital,' she repeated, with mounting urgency. 'You need to take me *right now*.'

'You're in shock and you're better off here. Rushing to the hospital isn't going to achieve anything. Right now, and for the next few hours, if not days, Alejandro will be out of it, undergoing a battery of tests. Trust me, I will be the first to know of any developments.'

Caitlin hesitated, soothed by his assertiveness. She realised that it had been a long time since someone else had taken charge and it felt good. 'I feel so helpless. He must be terrified.'

'Caitlin, he's in the equivalent of a deep sleep. He'll be as peaceful as a newborn.'

All that stress, she thought, riven with guilt. Yes, he'd fallen, but was a part of him retreating from the awkward situation he had obviously found difficult to cope with? Had his brain decided to conveniently shut down just for the moment?

There were so many cases of people forgetting traumatic events, relegating them behind closed doors in their head because they just couldn't cope with the memories.

Had Alejandro done the equivalent?

And yet, she thought feverishly, they had both been so cavalier about this arrangement.

Alejandro was gay. This was a revelation that had seeped out over a period of months and Caitlin had been more surprised at his shame at the admission than the admission itself. After all, in this day and age, who thought twice about someone being gay?

But she didn't understand, he'd said matter-of-factly. His background, generation upon generation of accumulated wealth, was mired in tradition, his elevated birthright an albatross around his neck.

He was the older and expected to marry and produce. It would kill his parents if they found out about his sexual persuasion. Nothing Caitlin had said over the months could assuage his anxiety but it was only when he told her that his parents were becoming increasingly vocal on the subject of his love life that she began to see just how much it was affecting his state of mind.

He'd begun playing truant from work. He'd stopped caring about whether his increasing absences were noted or not. If only his brother would get married, he'd told her. That would let him off the hook. He'd be able to remain free for longer, at least until he sorted out what he would do in the future. But Dante, he had said, just wasn't playing ball.

And his parents wanted to know what was going on. Why had they not been introduced to any girlfriends? They had someone in mind for him, a lovely girl, daughter of one of their friends. They were insistent on a meeting.

And from there, Alejandro and Caitlin's plan had been born.

He'd been desperate and so...had she.

She wasn't going to think of her own circumstances. This was about Alejandro and the fact that he was in hospital and she couldn't help but blame herself because she hadn't seen just how stressed he'd been at the whole mess and at lying to all his friends and family.

'Where are—what's happened to everyone?'

'Gone.'

'Gone?'

'Shuffled out in an orderly line. My parents went to the hospital but they've heeded the consultant's advice and returned to their place.'

'What is the prognosis?'

She'd been borderline hysterical but now her brain had re-engaged and she was a lot calmer. Dante's sense of calm was mesmerising and infectious.

'Excellent.'

'Would you lie to me?'

'Of course I would.' He smiled, and just for a second she understood how power, charm and incredible physical perfection could be an intoxicating mix.

Her heart picked up a beat and she suddenly felt hot and bothered.

'But,' he continued, still smiling, 'in this instance I'm not. Yes, there are broken bones, and it'll be a while before those completely heal, and, yes, he's been concussed, but all his vital signs are good and if he's out of it just at the moment, Roberto, the consultant who was here, has assured us that a full recovery is to be expected.'

'But you said that he's in a coma.'

'He's out of it at the moment, yes. Perhaps *coma* might be something of a dramatic term.'

'So how long do you think…does the consultant think…?'

'Can't put a timeline on it. Could be a day, could be a week. Doubtful that it'll be longer. All the signs are good.'

'That's such a relief.'

'It's a disappointing end to what should have been one of the best nights of your life,' Dante murmured, briefly lowering his eyes.

'Yes, it's a shame,' she returned politely as her mind hived off in other directions.

'You don't sound too distraught.'

'Of course I'm distraught.'

'You were certainly upset when he toppled over.' Dante was getting that feeling again, that vague, shadowy feeling that something didn't quite add up but he couldn't put his finger on *what exactly*. It was frustrating. In Dante's world, everything added up. There were no loose ends because he always made sure that there weren't any. He never asked himself whether he was missing out on the adventures that spontaneity could bring.

When he glanced back over his shoulder to the kid who had allowed himself to be carried away on the spontaneous adventure of straying out of his comfort zone with an older woman from a different background, it was like looking at a stranger. The stupid thing was that he knew that what he had felt at the time, and what had propelled him into throwing himself into his ill-advised affair, had had nothing to do with love. Infatuation, yes, and lust, most definitely, but that had been it. Everything else had stemmed from a defiant act of rebellion against a life that had been preordained from birth. Someone had to take the reins of the family empire and he had known, even then, that it probably wasn't going to be Alejandro.

How had he known that? Dante could only assume it was because his parents had begun, automatically, to turn to *him* for his opinions on the stock markets, on trends, on modernisation, *on the way forward*. Bound within the confines of this life, he had broken free in an act of rebellion that had cost him dearly and not just in terms of the money he had recklessly flung at the woman. His pride had been injured and he had glimpsed a vision of weakness inside him that had required eradication. He had shut down his emotions and ruthlessly taken control of every aspect of his life.

Vague, shadowy feelings didn't sit well with him. Neither did the way his body refused to obey his head when he looked at the pocket-sized redhead, who had no business getting under his skin the way she did. Her intentions were open to question and getting to the bottom of what she was up to with his brother was a straightforward matter. He would then respond accordingly.

So the jostle of unwelcome responses inside him that had nothing to do with the business of finding out what she was up to was an unwelcome reminder of a weakness he'd thought he had put to bed. It got on his nerves.

She wasn't lying when she said that she had, indeed, been distraught when his brother had hit the ground. She just didn't seem overly upset at the fact that he had hit the ground at their engagement party, thereby ensuring a premature and unwelcome conclusion.

Now that he thought about it, he couldn't remember her flashing the diamond ring at all. What excited bride-to-be didn't flash her engagement ring at her own engagement party?

He glanced at her finger. She was absently fiddling with the ring, slipping it off and on her finger, twisting it round and round. It was startlingly modest in its proportions.

Unwittingly, he looked at her, felt that tightening in his groin again.

'I knew he'd been overdoing it with the drink.' Caitlin spoke her thoughts aloud, eyes sliding away from Dante's over-the-top masculine presence. Her conscience still plagued her. This had been a terrible idea, an awful plan and she should have argued more against it, but she'd allowed necessity to override common sense, and now thinking about poor Alejandro, lying unconscious on some sanitised hospital bed in an impersonal, clinical hospital room, filled her with remorse.

'I should have done something about that. He's not used to drinking a lot. He's quite abstemious normally.'

'Yes, that's a curious one, isn't it?'

Caitlin looked at him. 'What are you talking about?'

'I did recall that my brother doesn't tend to hit the bottle hard. I just wondered why, of all nights, he should decide to sample every drink that went past him on a tray...'

He wasn't going to let up. That was the thought that ran through her head. There had been a lull in the attack amidst the chaos of Alejandro being rushed to hospital, and during that lull she had glimpsed another Dante Cabrera, but normal proceedings had resumed and he *just wasn't going to let up.*

The man was like a dog with a bone, and not just *any dog.* Nothing she could turn her back on and ignore. This dog with a bone wasn't a loveable poodle. He was a pit bull and he wanted to sink teeth into her until he prised every little secret out.

She had no intention of letting him do any such thing but her blood ran cold as she felt him circling her.

'Who doesn't feel nervous on an occasion like that?' she responded smoothly. '*I* was a bag of nerves. As you know.'

'You *were* concerned about your outfit,' Dante agreed. 'But, moving on from the troublesome subject of my brother's alcohol intake and his hospitalisation, the question is what happens from here?' He vaulted upright and paced towards the window, his movements as elegant and as stealthy as a jungle cat. He stared out for a few moments, then turned to look at her. 'Like I said, Alejandro probably won't come round for a day or two, but even when he does there's the business of those broken bones. He's going to be off his feet for some weeks, I would imagine…'

'He's going to go stir-crazy.'

'We can agree on that,' Dante said ruefully. 'Not that anything can be done to change that situation. On the upside, he'll be able to keep on top of work. Much of what needs to be done can be done via email and conference call. Thank God we live in a connected world.'

'He'll be thrilled to hear that,' Caitlin said sarcastically, without thinking, and then she flushed as Dante looked at her through narrowed eyes.

'You think he should refrain from working while he recuperates?'

'I think…' She shot Dante an accusatory look from under her lashes because she was now in the awkward position of having to explain what she had meant.

Didn't he know *anything* about his own brother? How was it possible for there to be such vast gaps between them? She'd never had siblings. When she was young, she'd *yearned* for one. It was heartbreaking, really, to witness a relationship that was so fractured.

'Yes?'

'I think…' she toed the middle ground '…he might appreciate a bit of peace from…er…the world of business…'

'What are you trying to tell me?'

He sounded genuinely perplexed and Caitlin sighed and decided to take a risk. A *tiny* risk. Wasn't it a starting point for these brothers to know a bit about one another? Alejandro, one day, would find the courage to explain who he was to his family and, when that day came, it would be so much smoother if Dante at least knew how his brother felt about working for the company.

'I'm not sure Alejandro is as…*besotted* with working for the company as you are…'

'Besotted?' Dante stared at her with rampant incredulity at yet another intrusion into areas of his life no one dared to explore.

'I know Alejandro tries to be as diligent as possible…' For Alejandro that actually meant working the minimum number of hours as efficiently as possible so that he could spend the remainder of his time exploring all those creative interests that he was more intrigued by.

Dante scowled and raked his fingers through his dark hair. 'I realise,' he conceded grittily, 'that he, perhaps, doesn't have the same drive as I have when it comes to running the company. Why do you think I've succeeded in diverging from the family business to build my own computer-software research companies? Because I've had nothing better to do? No, Alejandro doesn't have the same drive, but I've had no complaints from any of the directors…'

Personally, Caitlin was sure that that was because Alejandro was loved by everyone he met. He could put in an hour a day and she knew that everyone would be loath to report him. The fact was that he did his job perfectly well, if he was to be believed. He just didn't enjoy it and he spent as little time as possible there.

'No…well…it's just…' She breathed in deeply and decided, like a diver staring down at a very tiny pool of water miles below, to take the plunge. 'It's not that he doesn't have the same drive as you do. It's just that his heart has never really been in finance and business.'

Fulminating silence greeted this remark.

'He's really a creative soul,' she ploughed on while Dante watched her without saying a word, his face wiped of expression. 'That's why we get along so well. He's very interested in all aspects of photography. He loves exhibitions. He's even thinking about dabbling in a bit of sculpture or maybe even going for a course in woodwork...'

'Sculpture? *Woodwork?*'

'So you see he won't mind not being connected to the outside world while he recuperates.'

'Why would Alejandro not enjoy the work he does?' Dante demanded. 'He's never had the responsibility for any decision-making. I run everything. The buck stops with me. He has always had the easy ride of keeping the customers happy. What's not to like?' He flushed darkly. There was an admission there somewhere and he refused to shine a light on it. For once, the forbidding wall of privacy he had constructed around him revealed foundations that weren't as solid as he had thought.

He wanted to lock the discomforting thought away, but a series of connections were happening in his head that made him wonder whether the distance between him and Alejandro didn't hark back to that gradual alignment of responsibilities. Had there been something inside him that had resented the fact that he, although younger, had been the one to assume the reins of leadership without asking for it? Had that resentment spilled over, gradually, into the relationship he had with Alejandro?

The clear green eyes searching his lean, rigid face

made his jaw harden in proud rejection of any sign of weakness.

'Maybe you judge him the way you would judge yourself,' Caitlin suggested quietly. 'Maybe because *you* enjoy being a workaholic, he must also enjoy being a workaholic because you share the same genetic code. But that's not how it works.'

'No one *enjoys* being a workaholic,' Dante responded coolly.

'I've offended you. I'm really sorry.'

'Offended me?' Dante scowled. 'Don't flatter yourself, *querida*.'

Caitlin flushed as she recognised a kick in the teeth when it was delivered.

'You asked for my opinion,' she returned shortly. 'And I gave it to you. Forget I ever said anything. You said something about Alejandro being in hospital for some time to come. Is there any chance that he could be transferred to a hospital in London?'

'If my brother was miserable in his job, he should have said something to me. As for being besotted with work… This vast family estate won't run itself because I'd rather have fun lazing around and going on holiday.' Dante was annoyed that he couldn't give it up.

'That's not what Alejandro is about!'

'Duty demands that the business falls to the sons. As it stands, I have my own concerns that occupy much of my time. The family business is now just part of something bigger for me, even though our father no longer busies himself directly in its running. However, it is up to the pair of us to take up where he has left off. Would Alejandro rather abandon his obligations so that he can pursue a life of fun and enjoyment?'

'Your own concerns?' Caitlin had latched onto his phrase...*duty demands*. It gave her a very clear idea of why Alejandro was so loath to be open about his sexuality.

'My parents built their company on import and export. I have single-handedly brought it into the twenty-first century and it has become a gold mine, but it is overshadowed by my own computer-software empire.'

'So you work hard. But you volunteered for that, didn't you? You weren't content to just run the family business. You wanted your own, I guess because you enjoy that kind of ruthless, cut-throat lifestyle. Alejandro just isn't built along the same lines. And the reason he hasn't said anything...' she sighed but it was too late to start wondering whether she'd got in over her head with this conversation '...is because of this whole duty and tradition thing. He knows he has to join the family business whether he likes it or not but...'

'He's never uttered a word of complaint to me,' Dante said roughly. 'I could...work this out differently... I have been thinking of taking my computer business into a different area—the leisure industry always has room for improvement.' He frowned, padded across to a chair and sat down, stretching his legs out to the side. 'The wheels are in motion for me to take over a couple of boutique hotels in South America. There would certainly be scope for some creative advertising.'

'He would absolutely *adore* that.'

'This is something my brother should have brought to my attention. It's ridiculous that I have only found this out via a third party.'

'Maybe he was scared of disappointing,' she murmured. 'Haven't *you* ever been scared of disappointing?'

'Disappointing who?'

'I don't know. Your parents…your girlfriend…'

'To answer your question, no.'

Such self-assurance, Caitlin thought with a fascinated shiver. Little wonder Alejandro, so full of insecurities and doubts, had never thought to confide in his much more confident younger brother.

What must it be like to go out with a guy like Dante Cabrera? Personally, she had never been drawn to tough Alpha-male types but something feminine quivered inside her just for a moment at the thought of being with someone so absolutely in command. He was born to take charge and she remembered how that had made her feel when she had been frantic with worry earlier on. *Safe.*

Yet, he was willing to make concessions because, whatever his relationship with his brother, however distant they were from one another and however wildly different their personalities, he cared enough to try to see things from Alejandro's point of view.

He wasn't just a man of action. He was a listener. The problem was that Alejandro had never tried talking and Dante did not invite confidences.

'We were talking about the fact that Alejandro will be in hospital for a while,' Dante picked up the conversation from where they had left off before they'd gone down various byroads, 'and I couldn't help but notice that you travelled over here light.'

Caitlin looked at him with puzzlement because she wasn't sure where he was going with this.

'You're going to need clothes, so we have to decide how we're going to play this.'

'What are you talking about?'

'Well, you won't be returning to London for a while. Presumably your company will allow you suitable time off?'

'Time off?' Caitlin parroted.

'Alejandro is here and he won't be going anywhere any time soon.' He paused, giving her ample opportunity to see where he was heading with this.

How could she abandon her fiancé after the first night when he was lying in hospital, unconscious?

She blanched.

'I… I hadn't actually banked on spending much time over here…' *Or any at all, for that matter.* 'I don't know what the company policy is on…on time off for…for…'

'Compassionate leave? That does exist in your company, doesn't it?'

'Of course, but you know… I'm a freelance photographer… Yes, I'm employed by them, but I get called on to do various shoots and I'm paid accordingly…'

'That hardly sounds a satisfactory situation.'

'I'm working my way up. It's not something that happens overnight…'

'So…what…? They're going to quibble over giving you time off because the guy you plan on marrying is lying unconscious on a hospital bed in Spain? What kind of crackpot organisation are we talking about here?'

'It's a very reputable company!'

'Good, then that's all sorted. You'll have to call them first thing in the morning.'

'Yes, but…' She'd been standing on fairly solid ground but now a roller coaster had whipped past, scooped her up and she was in mid-air and travelling at speed.

'I'm not getting what the problem is here, Caitlin. Either you want to be with Alejandro or you don't. Which is it?'

'Of course, I would love to be around to make sure that he's going to be okay!'

Dante frowned. 'Good. Then let's not put unnecessary obstacles in the way. Back, though, to what I was saying earlier. You seem to have travelled over here with next to nothing. You'll need clothes. Do you want me to arrange to have some of yours brought over for you?'

'That won't be necessary,' Caitlin muttered. The

walls had well and truly closed in and there was no point trying to reconfigure the space. 'I expect if you point me in the direction of the nearest town, I'll be able to buy one or two things.'

Dante shrugged. 'I'd look at a fortnight here.'

'A fortnight...?' She tried not to sound appalled.

'And naturally, you will have to stay here.'

'Here?'

'Where else?' He raised his eyebrows and held her dismayed gaze. 'Unless you'd rather stay with my parents? They're not very handy for the hospital, but I'm sure they would not object to putting you up for however long you think you'll need to stay...'

'What? No!'

'Didn't think so. Not many brides-to-be would leap at the chance of staying with their in-laws, especially when they've only known their in-laws for a matter of a few hours.'

'I wouldn't want to impose,' Caitlin objected faintly, and Dante took his time looking round the huge sitting room with its high ceilings and sprawling bay windows. His dark eyes were cool and amused when they finally rested on her face.

'I wouldn't worry about it. I don't think we'll be bumping into one another because I live in a shoebox. Fact is, I doubt my brother would appreciate me turning you away at the door, given the circumstances.'

Caitlin, in her head, begged to differ. Alejandro would understand completely if she headed for the airport, clutching her bag. They were friends, after all, and certainly not the couple Dante assumed they were.

That said, if she ended up staying in Spain, he would also have sympathised with her perfectly reasonable desire to hit the nearest B & B because sharing space with Dante would be like sharing space with a hungry tiger on the prowl.

Realistically, though, was there any way that she could turn down the man's offer? He was already casting his net of suspicion far and wide.

'If it makes you feel any better, I'm rarely around. Naturally the staff will be here so you won't have to worry about anything at all. I know you'll be worried sick about Alejandro…but, rest assured, he is in the best hands, which I'm sure you know because you're certainly handling the shock better than I would have expected.'

He had vaulted to his feet and was heading for the door. She followed.

'What did you expect?' They were back in the body of the house and it was quiet. The army of staff who had scurried with their trays of champagne and caviar had had another role to fill and had removed all evidence of the party, so that now it was as though it had never been. A dream. Except…*not*.

'Well…' He spun round so suddenly that she almost crashed into him. She hastily stepped back and their eyes collided, startled green meeting cool, speculating midnight black. 'Call me stupid, but I thought there might be some hysteria involved.'

'Hysteria?'

'Naturally, you were clearly upset and shaken, but…let's just say I admire your self-control…'

'I'm not that type.' Caitlin licked her lips nervously.

'So it would appear,' Dante murmured lazily. 'I like that. And yet that seems to contradict the firecracker who attacked me outside the house.'

Caitlin flushed. How on earth was she going to manage spending a few *hours* here, never mind a few days?

He was so different from Alejandro. She wished her so-called erstwhile fiancé had told her a bit more about his forbidding younger brother. She might have, at least, come prepared. As things stood…

'No matter,' Dante said smoothly, spinning back on his heels and striding towards the curving staircase, one of two that dissected the mansion, 'we all have our different ways of dealing with distressing situations.'

'Where are we going?'

'Your rooms. Your bag will follow.'

He paused, pushed open a door and stood back so that she could precede him into a self-contained apartment that was the last word in luxury, from the thick velvet drapes to the rich Persian rug that partially covered the highly polished wooden floor. Through interlinking doors, she could see a sitting room.

'Thank you.' Gratitude didn't seem quite the emotion she was feeling. 'Please don't feel that you have to look out for me *at all*. I'll be more than capable of making my way to the hospital and into the town

while I'm here. I'll call work in the morning and find
out what sort of leave I'll be allowed…' His silence
was oppressive.

'No need to thank me.' He lowered his lashes,
shielding his expression, then looked at her. 'And
banish all thoughts of making your way anywhere.
I'll have a car waiting to take you to the hospital tomorrow and also to the town so that you can stock
up on clothes.'

'Of course.' How on earth was she going to afford a new wardrobe? How was any of this making
any sense at all? Why, why, why had they jumped
head first into water without first finding out how
deep it was?

'In the meantime…' he strolled towards the door
and lounged against the door frame for a few seconds, looking at her with a veiled expression '…try
and relax. Have a soak. By the time you're out of the
bath, your clothes will be here. And when it comes
to shopping? Buy a swimsuit. There's a superb infinity pool. I think you'll like it.' He straightened.
'When you're not agonising about Alejandro, kick
back a little. You'll be waited on hand and foot. You
may find that you won't be able to resist thinking of
it as an unexpected little holiday…'

CHAPTER FOUR

HOLIDAY? *HOLIDAY? WAS the man mad?*

Caitlin peered out of the sitting-room window and wondered which of the cars parked outside might be the one designated to take her into the city. Would she be summoned by someone? One of the members of staff? There was no helpful chap in a uniform poised by an open car door to offer her any clues and she wasn't quite sure what she should do.

She'd had a restless night as the consequences of what had transpired began to take shape in her head.

A week here. At the very least. Work, at any rate, had been sympathetic but she was new to the job and freelance so she didn't know just how long the sympathy would last.

Her parents had been puzzled.

'Spain? Why are you in Spain, darling? You never mentioned going on holiday…'

No, of course she hadn't! This fleeting visit was supposed to last a handful of hours, after which she would have been able to see a clear way forward with all the problems that had disastrously landed on her lap without warning.

Instead, here she was, peering out of a window and wondering what more disasters lay in wait.

Lost in her thoughts, she was unaware of footsteps behind her until she heard Dante's voice.

'Have you been waiting long? After last night's adventures, I thought you might want a lie-in.'

Caitlin spun round to see him lounging in the doorway. She'd expected an empty house. Dante had more or less reassured her that if she stayed under his roof, there would be almost no chance of them bumping into one another. The house was as vast as a castle and she had assumed that he would be out of it anyway, back working, but now she wondered how she could have been so naïve. Whatever brief periods of respite there had been since Alejandro's accident, Dante was still determined to piece her together and dig deep to find out what was going on.

She had to be on guard, but as she looked at him she knew that she would have to fight her own physical responses to him, which threatened to undermine her resolve at every turn. She couldn't work out how someone who made her hackles rise and threatened her peace of mind could have the sort of effect on her that he did. Was it because she just hadn't been interested in any guy since Jimmy? Or was it because she had always assumed that if she ever looked twice at another man, he would be in her league, someone reliable and grounded, someone *who made sense*.

There was no chance that she had caught him on his way out because he wasn't dressed for work. He was in a pair of black jeans and a black polo-necked shirt with a distinctive red logo on the pocket. He looked darkly, sexily *dangerous* and her nervous system went into immediate overdrive.

'I thought you would be at work,' she said, already on edge. 'I...er...wasn't sure what to do about transport into town.'

'You're looking at your transport.' Dante straightened and glanced at his watch.

'What are you talking about?'

'I've decided that it would be inappropriate to abandon you in your time of need. You don't know this part of the world, I'm guessing, and you're going to need someone to show you around while you're here.'

'Show me around?' Caitlin couldn't think of anything she needed less than Dante playing tour guide for the next few days. 'Why? Don't you have more important things to do?'

'What could be more important than making sure that my brother's beloved fiancée isn't left alone and floundering in a strange city? Come on. We can hit the hospital first, and then I will take you to the shopping district where you can buy sufficient clothes to tide you over.'

Caitlin quailed at the prospect of spending money she didn't have on things she didn't need.

Dante wasn't hanging around, waiting for any further protestations from her. He was already heading out of the sitting room and towards the imposing front door, barely leaving time for Caitlin to trip along behind him, clutching her knapsack.

The clean-up job on the house had been spectacular. As she was progressed along at fast speed, she could only guess that an army of helpers had been hard at it, wiping away all evidence of the elaborate party that had come to such a premature end.

It was not yet nine thirty and already it was hot outside.

Dante ignored all four cars parked in the massive courtyard and instead headed to the side of the house, beeping open a low-slung, steel-grey sports car that hadn't been visible from the sitting-room window.

He held open the passenger door for her.

Caitlin dropped into a plush leather bucket seat that made her feel as though she was inches away from making uncomfortable physical contact with the ground. Peering over the sleek walnut dashboard was a challenge because of her lack of height.

Dante, on the other hand, as he slid into the driver's seat and donned a pair of dark sunglasses, looked like a racing driver about to do a few winning laps around a circuit.

'Good news from the hospital,' he said as soon as the car revved to life. 'Alejandro is progressing well. He still hasn't regained consciousness, but all his vitals are good and those broken bones are the only damage he appears to have suffered. They can't work out how he lost consciousness and can only think that he must have dropped to the ground in a peculiarly awkward manner.'

'That's great,' Caitlin said with genuine warmth. 'Do we…er…have any idea how long he will be… out of it?'

'Absolutely none, but the signs are good for a speedy recovery on that front. I'm assuming you've contacted your people at work and been granted whatever time off you need?'

'I've phoned and told them that I will probably be here for about a week.' She braced herself for criticism.

Instead, Dante said smoothly, 'We'll head to the hospital first. You must be keen to see Alejandro.'

'Of course.' She noted the quick sideways glance Dante shot her but there was no way she could sound like a besotted lover, desperate to see her wounded fiancé.

Naturally, she was deeply concerned about what had happened and relieved that he had not had a more serious accident, given the wild abandon with which he had been drinking, but, much as she cared about Alejandro, he was, in the end, simply a very good friend and her pretence could only stretch so far. Not only would she have found it impossible to pretend to be loved up, but Alejandro would have had an even harder time of it.

It was just terrible luck that he happened to have

a brother with eagle-sharp eyes and the prowling, suspicious nature of a trained sniffer dog.

'I guess your parents must be so relieved…'

'Naturally. They'll be visiting later today and, of course, they will want to see you, make sure you're okay, even though I've already told them that you couldn't be better. Given the circumstances.'

Caitlin gritted her teeth together at the implied judgement call in that throwaway remark but she remained silent, taking in the change of scenery as the grand and leafy outskirts of the city were left behind and the car began to nose its way into the main area of the very beautiful city.

She had never been to Madrid before, never been to Spain, if truth be told, and her artistic eye fully appreciated the beguiling mix of old and new, high tech and historic, sleek glass and pastel coloured.

'And you are okay, aren't you?'

Reluctantly she dragged her attention away from the passing scenery and focused on the aristocratic profile of the guy sitting next to her, one hand on the steering wheel, the other resting lightly on the intimidating gearbox.

So different from his brother, she thought a little helplessly. Chalk and cheese had more in common. She just had no idea how to deal with him or how to handle herself when she was around him.

Everything about him made her nervous, from his aggressive good looks to his cool, watchful self-assurance.

'Of course.' She cleared her throat. 'How far is the...hospital from here? Once I know the route, I would be happy to make my own way in to visit.'

'How would you propose to do that?'

'There must be some form of public transport close to your house?'

'Sadly not.' He shot her a sideways look that carried a hint of amusement. 'Of course, I could always arrange for my driver to take you but, like I said, I feel personally responsible for your well-being while you are here. We're twenty minutes away from the hospital, by the way.'

Caitlin was so tempted to protest, yet again, that he had no need to feel responsible for her in any way, shape or form, but why bother? The man was determined to take her under his wing and she hadn't been born yesterday. She knew that if she was under his wing, he would be able to keep a sharp eye on her and would be in a prime position to keep prodding away, poking into nooks and crannies, airing his suspicions and waiting for her to slip up.

How long would it take for that to happen? she wondered. How long before she slipped up?

Not long. She wasn't used to lying. Manoeuvring through the labyrinth she and Alejandro had innocently created was going to take the dexterity of a magician.

As they approached the hospital she finally allowed herself to think about the convoluted road she was now travelling down.

It had all seemed so straightforward not that long ago. She would pretend to be Alejandro's fiancée, thereby buying him time from his parents, who were pushing for a solid relationship from their eldest son and the inevitable production line of much-wanted grandchildren.

He would pay her, he'd said.

Caitlin had adamantly refused. Not only could she not see the reason for such drama, but the thought of being paid for it was ridiculous.

But then circumstances had changed in a heartbeat for her, and Alejandro, who had not abandoned his plan despite her initial refusal to co-operate, had found a way past her defences.

She had no interest in his money for herself because she didn't have a materialistic bone in her body, but when her parents had become involved, her love and loyalty to them had very quickly become the quicksand that had begun to drag her under.

'I don't believe it,' she had poured her heart out to Alejandro one evening, several months earlier. 'How could Dad have lost everything? There are news bulletins all the time about scammers, but he's gone and lost everything, Alejandro! His savings, his pension. Gone. *Pouf!* They have the house, of course, but how on earth are they going to afford to support themselves as they get older?'

'What about your mum?'

She'd known that Alejandro would be grappling with the concept of having nothing. The backdrop to his life was paved with gold and priceless gems. He, literally, would have no concept of just how agonising it would be for two pensioners to realise that their life savings had gone. But he had sympathised as she had talked to him about the situation, told him that, as the only child, it fell upon her shoulders to build up some kind of nest egg for them so that they wouldn't be terrified of growing old in poverty.

And even then, it had been awful but within the realms of possibility until her lovely, kind and gentle mother had had a heart attack and they had all been told by the consultant that stress could prove to be a fatal enemy.

The conversation that had been left behind, Alejandro's offer to pay her generously for helping him out, had begun to beckon.

When he'd raised the subject again, Caitlin's defences had been in a different place.

She had listened.

It still went against the grain. She still didn't get why he couldn't just come right out and tell the world that he was gay.

But she had listened.

Just a couple of days, he had told her with bright and breezy confidence. A small bit of acting, a make-believe relationship, enough to convince his parents that they were involved.

No dates would be set for anything and they would return to London, where they would resume their lives and he would be granted a reprieve.

Once his brother had married, he had assured her, everything would change and the pressure would be off. And of course, he had told her earnestly, he would tell them all the truth. It would be easier then.

And the money…

He had named a sum that had made her eyes water. All her parents' problems would go away. It would be like waving a wand. Caitlin had thought of her mother and the possible horrendous consequences of another heart attack brought on by ongoing stress… She'd thought of her father, who would never forgive himself for getting them into the mess that he had… She'd thought of two lives that would end in tatters…

And Alejandro's proposal had suddenly seemed like manna from heaven. She had swept past her hesitation and doubt and she had agreed.

Except, she was here now, and nothing was straightforward any more…

Not when Dante was in the driving seat, which he was.

'We're here.'

Caitlin surfaced and stared at the sprawling glass building facing her, abuzz with activity, its harsh, clinical contours softened by thoughtful planting of trees and shrubbery in strategic places.

Like royalty, Dante dumped the car right outside the building and it was efficiently collected by someone she could only assume was his driver, who had been forewarned to meet them there.

He strode into the white brightly lit corridors of the hospital and crowds parted. He glanced neither left nor right. He led the way with certainty and she tripped along in his wake, profoundly relieved that he knew just where he was going and what he was doing.

She spoke absolutely no Spanish and she couldn't think how difficult everything would have been had she come here on her own.

He spoke in rapid Spanish to a consultant who had been summoned, and then finally turned to her.

'I appreciate that you must find all of this very confusing.'

'I'm glad you're here,' Caitlin admitted with a smile. 'I have no idea how I would have coped. I would probably still be in a taxi trying to get the driver to understand where I needed to go.'

Dante shot her a sideways glance. 'I'm surprised you don't know any Spanish at all, given the fact that you're engaged to a Spaniard.'

For once, there wasn't that jagged edge of suspicion underlying his remark. He sounded genuinely curious as they began to walk along the corridor to the room previously indicated by the consultant.

'Alejandro did try,' she admitted. 'It only took him five seconds to realise that he wasn't going to get anywhere when it came to me picking up a second language.'

'Not interested?'

'Very interested but my brain just doesn't seem equipped to handle it.' She laughed.

Dante's dark eyes slid over to her. That laugh... as infectious as her smile. Unconsciously he glanced down at her sexy, round curves, the softness of her fair skin, the vibrant colours of her copper hair, which she had tied back into something resembling an untidy bun. She smelled faintly of flowers and sunshine. There was something intensely appealing about her lack of artifice and that appealing *something* dragged on his senses, made him hyperaware of her in ways he knew he shouldn't be. He knew the dangers of *different*. He knew what shame and wounded pride tasted like and he knew that the road that led there started with irrational temptation. It had that one and only time. It was a road he was never going to walk down again. On so many levels, the woman standing here was wrong and yet...

When he thought of the sort of woman he was destined for, a woman like Luisa, other thoughts pushed their way through, discomforting, uncontrollable thoughts that had no place in his life. Of course, he would never go there. He was supremely confident when it came to his ironclad willpower, but the mere fact that he couldn't stop his mind from wandering rankled.

'Somewhere along the line, I think my parents gave up on me being academic and so, in my head, I just ended up assuming that I couldn't do anything

that wasn't creative. Hence my love of art and photography.'

'You should learn.'

'Why?'

'It might come in useful,' Dante interposed drily.
'Considering the circumstances.'

Caitlin laughed again. 'Oh, Alejandro and I won't
be…' She went scarlet and came to a grinding stop.

'Won't be *what*?' Dante encouraged softly, his
ears pricking up.

'Nothing,' Caitlin muttered. How could she have
let all her defences drop with him? How had she
managed to let that charm get under her skin and
very nearly pull the rug from under her feet?

He was staring at her. She could feel the insistence of his eyes boring into her skin and she pur-
posefully kept her head averted and, thankfully, they
had landed up outside Alejandro's room so she had a
very good excuse to ignore the guy towering next to
her so that she could focus on her supposed fiancé,
who was lying on the bed, for all the world looking
as if he just happened to be in a deep sleep.

As peaceful as a baby, she thought, leaving her to
deal with the fallout on her own.

'If it's okay, I'll go see him…on my own, if you
don't mind.'

Dante didn't mind. He was still trying to work out
what she had just said. It had slipped out and she had
immediately regretted the oversight. He knew that
and it wasn't just because she had gone a beetroot-red

shade of intense discomfort, the intense discomfort of an adult who had very nearly broken the tidings to a gullible four-year-old that Santa wasn't real. He had *sensed* it, had sensed her horror at something that had very nearly been said.

What was it, though?

He was excellent when it came to reading people and reading, more importantly, what was between the lines. It was a talent he had ruthlessly exploited over the years, because it had always given him the upper hand when it came to the cut and thrust of dealmaking.

You never made it far by believing anything anybody said to you. He certainly never trusted anyone unless they had gone the distance to earn it. Few ever had.

Dante believed every word Caitlin had told him about her relationship with his brother, namely that they went back a way and had started out as great friends. He could see the *friend* bit clearly enough. It was what she *omitted* to say he found so intriguing, and that near slip-up she had narrowly escaped had compounded his suspicions.

She'd hurried into the room, closing the door behind her, and he watched through the pane of glass in the door as she pulled a chair closer to the bed and sat down, taking one of Alejandro's hands in hers for a quick pat and then leaning forward to talk.

There was no gentle caressing of the brow or tender kiss on the mouth, and after that perfunctory pat she had dropped his hand with shameless speed.

He would have given his right arm to have been a fly on the wall because, whatever she was saying, it didn't appear, reading her body language from behind, that she was soothing him with sweet nothings.

Dante spun round and was helping himself to some drinking water from a plastic cup when she approached to briskly thank him for delivering her.

'I can make my way to the shops from here,' she said firmly. 'We're in the centre of things. I won't need you to traipse behind me. If you want to visit with Alejandro, I can either meet you back here or else I'll grab a taxi to the house.'

'How did you find him?'

'He seems comfortable enough.' She sincerely hoped he'd heard every word she'd said when she'd told him in no uncertain terms that he'd been an idiot to have consumed his body weight in champagne and that she was really out of her depth having to cope with Dante, who watched her so closely that she felt uncomfortable every time she drew breath.

'Honestly, Alejandro,' she'd all but wailed, 'what on earth possessed us?' She wondered whether she had imagined the flicker of his eyes when she had said that. If he could hear her, then he was probably trying hard to blink in agreement.

'Wait here. I will come to the shops with you. You're about to tell me that there's no need but I wouldn't bother to waste my breath if I were you.

You're new to Madrid and it's the very least I can do.'
Under any other circumstances, Dante would have
spent fifteen minutes with his brother and then continued on to his high-rise office in the city centre to
pick up where he had left off on the work front, but
the green-eyed, butter-wouldn't-melt-in-her-mouth
redhead, trying not to look appalled, suddenly made
all things work-related fade into the background.

'Fine.' Caitlin shrugged and took a seat outside
the room and waited. For the first time, something
loomed even more stomach-churning than the prospect of Dante lurking like a hangman's noose, and
that was the thought of a shopping expedition she
couldn't afford.

He wasn't long. Ten minutes at the most. Well,
she thought, they barely had anything to say to one
another when Alejandro was on top form, so lying
unconscious on a hospital bed wasn't exactly going
to be conducive to a lengthy visit.

'That was quick.' She'd aimed for sarcasm. She
ended up with compassion because it was sad. Dante
looked at her, his handsome face darkly rejecting
the soft empathy in her voice and yet…as he raked
his fingers through his hair and continued to stare,
the atmosphere suddenly shifted. He wasn't retali-
ating, calling her to account, slamming the door in
her face. He looked lost for words and, in that moment, intensely human and vulnerable.

'I'm sorry,' she said softly, reaching to rest her
small hand on his arm.

'I don't do pity.'

'I'm still sorry. I always longed for a sibling but it wasn't to be. I'm sorry for both of you that, as brothers, you've drifted so far apart.'

'These things happen.'

'They do,' Caitlin agreed. Their eyes were locked and she had unconsciously stepped a bit closer towards him. 'But there's usually a reason behind it. I'm sad for you both because you seem to have just drifted into silence. It's crazy.'

'Not crazy,' Dante said roughly. 'In a busy life, things can sometimes drift. My fault. My brother's fault. Who knows? I agree...it's...not ideal.'

Caitlin smiled. 'Not how I would have described it...'

Dante smiled back. 'That's because you're emotional and I'm not.'

The silence that fell was brief, thrumming with something he couldn't put his finger on and broken when a woman said, from behind, 'Sorry, but am I breaking something up here?'

Dante spun round and Caitlin expelled a long breath and blinked at the leggy brunette staring at them with narrowed, assessing eyes.

'Luisa.' Dante pushed himself off the wall, his brain failing to instantly engage. It was sufficiently engaged, however, to bring home to him that Luisa was the last person he had any interest in seeing. She had been hard work at the aborted party the evening before, trying desperately to revive a relationship that was well and truly in the throes of rigor mortis. 'What are you doing here?'

Luisa pouted. 'I've come to see your brother, Dante. What else?' Her eyes were chips of diamond-hard ice as they briefly settled on Caitlin, who was fervently wishing that she could be anywhere but here. Deliberately eliminated from the conversation, she could only hover, acutely uncomfortable at being third wheel in whatever drama was unfolding between Dante and the other woman.

'I popped in to have a chat with your parents…' Luisa half turned, drawing Dante into a private huddle with her. 'They're so worried but I reassured them that Alejandro will be just fine.' She smiled broadly and lightly rested her hand on Dante's shoulder, making small stroking movements against the sleeve of his polo shirt. 'Maybe…' the smile was coquettish now and she had lowered her voice to a husky murmur '…you and I could go somewhere and grab a coffee? Maybe some lunch? That lovely little place we went to a few months ago would be perfect…'

'Did my mother happen to mention that I would be here?'

Luisa laughed nervously.

'No coffee, Luisa,' he said on an impatient sigh. 'No lunch. I'm heading into town. Caitlin needs clothes because she will be staying on. I am taking her shopping.' He glanced down at Caitlin and Caitlin saw a flash of venom cross Luisa's perfect face, gone in a heartbeat, replaced with a gentle smile of understanding.

'You're such a gentleman, Dante.' Luisa forced the smile in Caitlin's direction and flicked some non-existent fluff from her figure-hugging dress before shaking her hair and throwing back her shoulders. 'Of course, you must look out for your brother's fiancée, seeing that she has no one here at the moment and must be grief-stricken at what's happened. I'm sure I'll see you when things settle down.'

During this interchange, Caitlin hadn't said a word and she didn't as she and Dante both left the hospital and made their way into the bustling city.

CHAPTER FIVE

THERE WAS NO WAY to be polite and beat about the bush so Caitlin took the bull by the horns and said, bluntly, 'Is there some kind of market I could go to?'

She was discovering that going anywhere on foot was unacceptable to Dante. He had driven his sports car directly to the hospital, where it had been collected by his driver. She guessed it had been returned to the house, because no sooner were they out of the hospital and standing outside in baking heat than another car showed up, this time a black four-wheel drive with darkly tinted windows.

She was bundled into blissful cold and immediately turned to him to repeat her question.

'Why would you want to go to a market?' He frowned. 'Special dietary requirements? Tell me and I'll instruct a member of staff.'

'Not a food market, Dante. A flea market where I can buy clothes.'

'It's false economy buying cheap tat,' Dante returned smoothly. He spoke to his driver in rapid Spanish and she lapsed into fretful silence as they were driven to and deposited on a tree-lined avenue where elegant buildings with discreet pale awnings advertised a range of exclusive designer stores. Gucci rubbed shoulders with Louis Vuitton and Jimmy Choo, and some names she didn't recognise looked even more upmarket.

'Dante!' She turned to him with desperation as she was hustled out of the car to find herself on the pavement. 'I can't afford to shop in a place like this!'

'You're engaged to my brother.'

'What does that have to do with anything?' She literally had a vision of fifty-pound notes blowing away from her savings account.

'This is a ridiculous conversation. I can't believe my brother would not spend money on you.'

'I prefer to spend my own money buying my own clothes,' she retorted angrily. 'What sort of world do you live in, Dante? No, forget I said that! You enjoy throwing money at the women you go out with because it's easier than the other option!'

'You're crossing lines.' His jaw hardened. 'Be careful.'

'Or else what?' Caitlin rolled her eyes and placed her hand belligerently on her hips. 'Dante, it's easier to spend money than it is to spend quality time, isn't it?'

Dante flushed with outrage. 'More tête-à-têtes with my brother about me?'

'No! I'm just observant. I can see that Luisa is besotted with you but it's not returned—and, yes,

Alejandro did say that you weren't keen on the notion of settling down.'

'Nor, presumably, is he, or he would have done it sooner.'

'It doesn't matter.' She sighed. 'I don't like accepting stuff from guys. It doesn't feel right. And I can't afford to buy anything in any of the shops on this fancy street.'

This was a first for Dante. The idea that a woman might resent having presents lavished on her puzzled him. What she viewed as some kind of insult to her feminism, he saw as an expression of appreciation.

'Caitlin, you're going to be here for at least a week. Who knows? Maybe longer. If you can't afford to spend money on yourself, then allow me. I do so on behalf of my brother. He can pay me back in due course, if it makes you feel easier. I hear what you're saying about not wanting to accept anything from anyone, but I feel that Alejandro would not want to think of you traipsing down to the local flea market. You're going to be entering a whole new dynamic when you marry my brother. Why not start adapting now? Besides, the flea market only opens on a Sunday.'

'Because people get engaged doesn't automatically mean they're going to get married,' Caitlin said vaguely. She realised that the deeper she dug her heels in, the odder it would seem to a guy like Dante, who lived in a completely different world from her.

Alejandro shared that world. He would lavish gifts on whatever partner he ended up with.

She wasn't going to win this one.

'I suppose Alejandro—'

'Good.' He spun round on his heels and swept her along to a shopping experience she hadn't banked on.

This was how the other half lived. She'd seen it on a grand scale in his mansion. The priceless artwork, the acres of polished marble, the invisibility of his staff paid to make his life as fuss-free as possible.

For the next three hours, she experienced it first-hand when it was exclusively directed at her.

He had chairs brought for him so that he could sit, his veiled expression revealing very little as clothes were fetched and carried. When money was no object, the attentiveness of the various boutique owners was ingratiating. They fawned and scurried and couldn't do enough.

And something deep inside Caitlin responded with a feminine enjoyment that was shameful because it just wasn't her.

Even before everything with her parents had fallen apart, plunging her into a financial nightmare, spending money on expensive clothes had never been her thing. Maybe it was her shape. In her head, expensive clothes were designed for a certain type of figure, one she didn't possess. Maybe it was the way she had been brought up. Her parents had always been sensible with money because they'd never had a great deal of it and it was an attitude that had been passed down to her.

Shopping with Dante Cabrera was not a sensible experience. The opposite. He snapped his fingers and people hastened to please. She was the beneficiary of his largesse and it was *thrilling*. She didn't want it to be, but it was.

Silk and soft cottons were laid for her inspection. The finest leather was brought out on show. She had had to resist the temptation to lovingly stroke some of the items of clothing.

'If you want an objective opinion,' Dante had drawled, standing next to her in that very first exclusive boutique, when the glamorous woman in charge had hurried off to find the right size for a dress Caitlin had guiltily admitted to really liking, 'then feel free.'

'No, thank you,' she had responded politely. But she had still *felt* his presence as he'd accompanied her on the shopping trip, had found her mind wandering back time and again to those dark, hooded eyes, his lean beauty, to the insane appeal of his lazy self-assurance.

His driver took bags of shopping to the car, patiently waiting wherever they happened to be.

It was exhausting and exhilarating at the same time and then, when it was over, when they were being ferried back to the house with half a store in the boot of the car, Dante murmured, softly, 'You should wear something you bought today to visit my parents. I accepted an invitation on your behalf. They're concerned about you…'

On a high from shopping, from breaking out of her comfort zone, temporarily freed from the unending stress of the past few months when every penny had had to be counted and allocated to a fund for her parents, Caitlin nodded. Yes. Why not? What was wrong with feeling like a living, breathing woman again? Just for an evening?

Dante's low-slung Ferrari glided through the iron gates, which opened silently at the press of a button.

It was mid-afternoon. He should still be at his glass high-rise in the Silicon Valley just outside the city centre.

Why was he here, driving up the tree-lined avenue towards his house?

Of course, he knew why. He hadn't been able to focus. He hadn't been able to focus for the past three days.

That shopping expedition…

Dante had been shopping with women before. He had always taken his laptop because, in between watching the inevitable parade of outfits, he had always been able to catch up on his emails as he'd positioned himself on a chair, in for the long haul.

He enjoyed lavishing presents on the women he went out with. Why not? He had more money than he knew what to do with. And women enjoyed being treated like queens.

Caitlin had not been one of them. Her remark about him throwing money at women because money was an easier sweetener to dish out than time and commitment had rankled. As far as he was concerned, it wasn't a case of one or the other. It was a case of him not being interested in commitment but enjoying being lavish. How were the two connected? He had refused to rise to the bait and had been outraged at yet another foray from the woman into his private life, which was and always would be out of bounds. She had accepted, finally, his offer to cover the cost of a new wardrobe, seeing that she was stuck in Spain, but he had then to persuade her that the purchase of cheap plastic shoes and disposable tat was out of the question.

What sort of man was Alejandro? he had privately questioned. Stingy? Surely not. He might not be on familiar terms with his brother, but stinginess didn't run in their family. So how was it that the woman he planned on marrying had to dip into her own pocket for essentials?

Dante knew that some might call him a dinosaur for thinking like that but he really didn't care. It was how he was, and he was shocked that his brother was not cut from the same cloth.

Accustomed as he was to the twirling of women as they tried on clothes, their insistence that he stay put so that he could give his opinion, Dante had been perversely fascinated by Caitlin's lack of interest in what he thought of her choices. Made sense, he knew, because it wasn't as though they were involved on any level, but he had still found himself dumping the laptop and watching what she went for even though there were no trying-on performances.

The three exclusive shops he took her to didn't offer anything he figured she would automatically make a beeline for. Nothing baggy. Nothing made from fabric better employed for curtains. Nothing designed for women who didn't want their bodies on show.

He'd found himself curiously keen to see the transformation and he had that very evening when he had stood there at the bottom of the stairs, glancing at his watch and waiting for her to emerge.

The dress she had worn to the ill-fated engagement party had revealed a figure she was at pains to hide. She had looked good but had clearly been ill at ease in it. The silk culottes and little matching silk vest she had worn to his parents' were much more her thing. She felt confident in them and that confidence spilled over into the way she moved, the way she carried herself, the way she walked. Did she imagine that, because they didn't cling to every inch of her, her figure was, somehow, less on display? If so, she was very mistaken. Knockout.

That was three days ago. The fierce pull of temptation had set alarm bells jangling in his head and he had dealt with the situation immediately. In between taking her daily to see Alejandro, he had cocooned himself away in his office at home and worked. He had told her that without the distractions that cropped up when he was accessible in his high-tech glass office, which was located some distance away from Madrid, in the equivalent of Silicon Valley, he could power-work and be at hand for any emergencies that might crop up at the hospital. They had met over dinner, prepared and left ready for reheating by one of his staff. They had made pleasant conversation about Alejandro, her job, the weather and various other bland topics. He had done his utmost to keep his eyes off her but, having told himself that she was out of bounds, he had been even more tempted to look.

He had noted the swing of her hips when she had carried her plate to the sink. He had been drawn to the fullness of her mouth every time she smiled. She had a tiny waist and that was apparent in the outfits she had bought—soft khaki shorts…a small denim skirt…a strappy dress with buttons down the front.

How could a man concentrate on work-related issues when the temptation of the forbidden had taken up residence in his head?

He had gone into his offices first thing that morning and had packed it in as soon as his meeting was over.

It was Friday. It was hot. He couldn't think straight. The constant interruptions had been getting on his nerves.

Made sense to return to his house and bury himself in his office as he had done previously. At least he wouldn't have to deal with his office door opening and shutting every three seconds.

So here he was. The simmering, dark excitement that seeped into his veins at the thought of seeing her was easy to dismiss as just the irrational pull of what was banned. The dangerous desire to hear her voice and indulge in those invigorating verbal sparring matches was a little more difficult to dismiss but Dante had every confidence in his capacity for self-control.

It was what made him the man he was today. No one ever rose to the top by allowing emotion to get the better of them and Dante, who had started with the sort of privileges most could only dream of, had risen to the very top, expanding his empire beyond belief, because of his ability to detach, his ability to suppress emotion in favour of cool-headed logic.

Cool-headed logic dictated that whatever temptations Caitlin posed, they were little more than titillating distraction in his high-powered but otherwise predictable life.

And anyway, he still wanted to find out what was going on with the woman, what the deal was between her and his brother, whether anything had to be severed before problems could arise.

So all in all...yes, it made complete sense to be returning home on a hot, sunny Friday afternoon...

From her bedroom window, Caitlin could appreciate the stretch of stunning manicured lawns, the clever array of trees that cast just the right amount of shade in just the right places. Facing towards the back of the house, she could almost delude herself into thinking that she was on holiday in some vastly expensive enclave for the super rich.

Dante was out of the house. She knew that because he had been leaving for work when she had descended that morning and had politely quizzed her about her plans for the day. His driver would be available, he had informed her, should she wish to go anywhere. He had already given her the guy's mobile number and she knew that, should she text Juan, a car would be ready and waiting to deliver her to any destination within seconds. When the wealthy snapped their fingers, people jumped to attention.

Were she on holiday, she now thought, stifling a sigh, then her head wouldn't be constantly buzzing with anxiety.

For the past few days, in between hospital visits and, on that one occasion, seeing Alejandro's parents for dinner, and generally trying to deal with Dante's unsettling presence, Caitlin had busied herself trying to sort out various stays of execution on loans she had discovered her parents had taken out, which they could no longer service. The deeper she dug into her parents' finances, and dig she did, the more rot she was discovering.

She communicated with her office but had already lost one job because she wasn't around to take it on.

She felt their sympathy was not going to be limitless and her frustration was growing by the hour.

Dante had told her, on that very first evening, when Alejandro's fall had put paid to their carefully made plans, that when she wasn't worrying, she should see her stint out in Spain as a little holiday.

Caitlin had never heard anything quite so ludicrous but now, with the sun burning down on a vision of impeccable greenery outside the bedroom, in which she was trying vainly to concentrate on collating various archive photos for a project she had been working on for the past six weeks, she felt suddenly restless.

She had had eight months of unimaginable stress. She had functioned in her job, had tackled the problems thrown at her, had dealt with the horror of her mother's poor health in the wake of their financial woes, and she'd thought she was doing fine, all things considered.

But sitting here now, she felt that perhaps she wasn't. She felt weary, as weary as a hundred-year-old woman. Not only was she now anxious about Alejandro, but she feared she might lose her job if she stayed out here much longer and then where would that leave her? And her parents? She had worked out a repayment schedule for the loans with the intention of saving as much as she could to stockpile a little cash for them. What on earth would she do if she didn't have a pay cheque coming in? She certainly couldn't accept a penny from Alejandro, considering the outcome to what they had planned had crashed and burned.

Amongst the various items she had bought, there was also a swimsuit because, yes, she had seen the pool, and it had looked inviting and, besides, the swimsuit was the least wildly luxurious of all the items of clothing she had purchased. Two bits of stretchy black cloth.

Temptation beckoned. Dante wasn't around.

The house was vast and yet it still felt as though she saw too much of him when they were both in it. She tried to keep their conversation basic and polite whenever they crossed paths, but it seemed he had the knack of dragging confidences out of her because she always had to fight to stay true to the role she had taken on board, and not let her guard down.

When he fastened those dark, speculative eyes on her it was almost as though she were being slowly dragged into a vortex and she had to physically keep her distance from him just to hang on to some self-control.

Did he notice? She hoped not.

What mattered was that there would be no dark, speculative eyes on her now. She had her window. Why not take advantage of it?

What else was she going to do? Think about all her problems and marvel that there was no way forward? Get depressed? Caitlin snapped shut her computer and headed for the chest of drawers to rifle through her meagre belongings for the bikini, which still had the tags on.

She changed quickly. She made her way down to an empty house. Everything that required doing had been done, and, in fairness to Dante, he was generous about letting his staff head home once their work was finished. It was Friday and the house was silent. Staff gone.

The unspoken rider to his generosity was that, should he discover any job half-done, then there would be all hell to pay. Caitlin assumed that that would be what he brought to the table in the work environment, as well. Total fairness. Big rewards for those who worked hard and deserved it but ruthless dispatch for those who failed to meet his standards.

She accessed the back garden through the kitchen door, which was spotless. There were always fresh flowers in a vase on the kitchen table and a balmy breeze lifted the muslin panels at the windows.

The scent of the flowers in the vase mingled with the smell of sunshine from outside and for a few moments the constant weight resting on her shoulders lifted, leaving her, for once, feeling like the young woman she was. Twenty-five, just, without a care in the world. The way it should be. Fresh in a job, going out with friends, with maybe a boyfriend in tow, and a future stretching out in front of her that promised everything even if, in the end, it fell short on delivery. Carefree. Happy.

Dante had told her that she should accept her enforced stay in Spain and enjoy it as a holiday rather than an inconvenience. He had said that with barely contained sarcasm as he had circled her like a shark in a small tank, letting her know that he suspected her motivations and would find her out in his own sweet time. At the time, Caitlin could think of nothing more unlikely than enjoying a second of her stay in Spain under his roof, but it was so glorious outside and she was so tired of being worn down and anxious.

The pool was wonderful, by far her favourite bit of the estate. It was crystal clear, a flat blue infinity pool flanked by decking that was slip proof but cleverly fashioned to look like glass. Around it, there was a veritable plethora of shrubbery. Flowers in the brightest hues of orange and yellow mingled with the deepest greens of leaves and ferns, and strategically positioned trees provided shelter from the sun, rather than umbrellas. It was like a lake within a park.

Out here was tranquil in a way the inside of the house never seemed to be. Even when there was no one to be seen, she was always conscious of the fact that there were housekeepers in the vicinity, cleaning and polishing and preparing food and making sure that life was as easy as possible for the master of the house.

Out here though…

Troublesome cares drained away as she basked in the sun, slowly relaxing and letting the accumulation of problems seep away. The water was wonderfully cool and she swam lazily, up and down, up and down, getting into a rhythm.

Her eyes were half closed, her breathing even when she surfaced at the deep end of the pool, blinked water out of her eyes and realised that someone was standing directly above her, casting a long shadow over the crystal-clear water.

Dante.

His towering figure took shape as she blinked into the dazzling sun, shielding her eyes.

She clung to the side of the pool, heart suddenly hammering.

He was in swimming trunks and a tee shirt and barefoot and he looked spectacular.

Her mouth went dry and she couldn't think of anything to say, although, roaring through her head, was the single thought... *Shouldn't you be somewhere else?*

And if he was here...why wasn't he dressed in a suit and tie, on his way to a meeting somewhere? Why was he in swimming trunks?

'Thought I'd join you,' Dante answered the question she'd been asking herself. He looked at the pool, the calm perfect blue. He hadn't been in it for months. Longer. No time. But today, heading down the corridor to his bedroom to have a shower, he'd happened to glance through the long window on the landing and seen her. She'd been swimming, taking her time, her long hair streaming out behind her. He'd abandoned work early. The woman had put a spell on him and he knew that he had returned to the house because he'd wanted to see her.

He told himself that she was an enigma and that could only be a bad thing when it came to the situation between her and his brother. With Alejandro laid up in a hospital bed, Dante would have time to solve the riddle of what, exactly, was going on between the pair of them and take whatever steps were necessary. He could be decisive.

She was hiding *something*. Whatever happened to be going on between her and his brother, it wasn't a passionate and loving relationship between two people desperate to tie the knot.

So what was it? If Dante could excuse his preoccupation with her as the natural outcome of wanting to protect the Cabrera dynasty from a potential intruder, he would have. However, she failed to conform to the one-dimensional cardboard-cut-out image he would have liked.

She was witty, sharp and disrespectful. She should have been desperate to curry favour with him, to get him onside if her plan was to marry his brother and then set herself up in the enviable position of being able to lay claim to the family fortune. Her mission seemed to be the opposite. She was either ostensibly avoiding him or else openly arguing with him.

She fascinated him because she was so different from all the women he went out with and because he just couldn't work out what was going on with her.

So when he had glanced through that window and

spotted her, he hadn't stopped to think. He'd headed straight to his bedroom, rummaged and found his swimming trunks, stuck on an old tee shirt, grabbed a towel and headed for the pool.

And here he was.

And there she was. Looking up at him, her face still wet, her hair dark from the water and fanning out around her like something from a pre-Raphaelite painting.

He hardened, felt that ache in his groin. He wondered whether coming down here had been the best of ideas. Maybe not.

'It's a hot day,' he muttered roughly, turning away to strip off the tee shirt and then diving with fluid grace into the pool, only to surface and shake his head before raking his fingers through his wet hair.

Caitlin edged back in the water. 'I wouldn't normally have come in...but...'

'Don't apologise, Caitlin. I'm glad it's being used. It's maintained twice weekly and yet so seldom used that I can't imagine why I had it put in in the first place.'

She could feel her cheeks burning. She was very much aware of him barely clothed, his body so close to hers that she could reach out and touch him with no effort at all.

He was so beautiful.

Seeing him here, bare-chested, she realised that, somewhere deep in her subconscious, she had wondered what he might look like underneath his expensive gear.

He lived up to expectation. Broad-shouldered, narrow-hipped, his torso the right side of muscular. There was a strength to his physique that made her think that he could pick her up one-handed and not feel the strain.

Plus, he wasn't asking those questions, those vaguely pointed questions that always made her so uncomfortable and guarded and on the defensive.

He was being *nice*.

'Why did you, in that case?' she asked, looking at him briefly, eyes locking, before spinning away and swimming towards the shallow end of the pool because all of a sudden she had to escape the stranglehold of his presence.

He followed her. He covered the length of the pool in slow, lazy strokes and somehow ended up by her side without looking as though he'd expended any energy at all.

'I had the entire place renovated when I bought it years ago.' He picked up the conversation where he had left off, as though there had been no interruption. 'The architect and designer at the time both agreed that a swimming pool would be an asset.' He shrugged. 'It's very ornamental.'

'But as you say, if it's not used…'

'Maybe somewhere, at the back of my mind, I had high hopes of using it now and again.' He smiled ruefully and a tingle of heated awareness shot through her body, making her fidgety and uncomfortable.

'But then what happened?'

'Really want to know?'

Caitlin nodded. She was uncomfortable with the conversation because it felt strangely intimate, and yet she wasn't sure why she should feel uncomfortable because they weren't sharing secrets and he wasn't telling her anything he probably hadn't told lots of people who might have asked the same question she had. And yet...

'I never seemed to find the time. Alejandro went to London but here, in Madrid—this is the heartbeat of the company, and not just the family business, but all the other networks I have subsequently developed on my own. The heart never stops beating and I am in the centre of it. Finding time to use this pool became an empty wish.'

'You sound trapped,' Caitlin mused, looking at him with empathy before turning away to sit on the step. 'I always got the impression that there was nothing you enjoyed more than working.'

Dante lowered his eyes, his lush, sooty lashes brushing his high cheekbones. He seldom, if ever, had conversations like this with any woman but he was enjoying talking to her, enjoying her calm intelligence, her refusal to kowtow to him and, most of all, the fact that she wasn't flirting with him, doing her utmost to grab his attention by flaunting her assets.

She wouldn't be, though, would she? She was

engaged to his brother. It was a reminder that was grudgingly acknowledged. She didn't act like someone who was engaged, but why did he constantly catch himself overlooking it? Was it a Freudian slip? Since when was he the sort of man who suffered from such weaknesses? After that one and only youthful error of judgement, from which lessons had been learnt, he had led a gilded life, where success after success had made him untouchable and given him an unshakeable confidence in his ability to control his destiny, so he was ill at ease with the fact that there were gaps in his armour he had never suspected.

'I'm far from trapped.' Was he, though? For one piercing second he envied the freedoms his brother enjoyed. He had an easy show to run, working in an office that was so well oiled he was barely needed at all, free to pursue just the sort of interests that had brought him into contact with the woman sitting next to Dante. He wondered whether there was a low-level, unconscious resentment that had fuelled the distance between himself and Alejandro.

Had he taken time to explore that possibility, was there a chance the chasm between them might have been bridged? And how was it that a stranger had been the one to propel him towards realisations he had barely acknowledged?

Caitlin shrugged and looked away. She was so intensely aware of him and the potency of his masculine appeal that she could scarcely keep her thoughts straight. She didn't trust herself to have the normal, inoffensive conversation the situation required.

Dante was finding her lack of interest in pursuing that tiny morsel of information thrown to her oddly annoying.

'And you?' he asked gruffly, shifting uncomfortably because he couldn't seem to look at the woman without his body misbehaving.

'What about me?' Caitlin raised her eyebrows with a slight frown.

'Do you feel trapped in the road you're going down? What's life like for you and my brother? What do you do together?'

Caitlin blushed. *What do good pals do*, she wanted to put to him, *except hang out together, listen to each other's woes, meet up as part of a group...?*

The charade stuck in her throat and for a few seconds she didn't say anything, but he was watching her, waiting for a response, and so she said, eventually, 'The usual.'

'The usual? What's that? Tell me?'

'What do *you* usually do with someone you're going out with?' Caitlin threw the question back at him, flustered.

'I wine them, I dine them, I shower them with whatever they want...'

'And then you dump them?' Caitlin was thinking of Luisa, the desperate yearning in her eyes when she had looked at him at the engagement party and the vicious jealousy when she had seen them together at

the hospital, chatting. Was that how he handled all
the women he dated?

Caitlin took a deep breath. The hot sun made her
feel reckless and daring. The intimacy that was sending shivers up and down her spine was unfurling
something dangerous inside her and suddenly she
was fed up of tiptoeing around the danger. If the
shark was going to attack, then why not weather the
attack now?

'You're suspicious of me, aren't you? You think
I'm after his money.'

'And if I am?'

'I don't know why you would be. What have I
done to deserve your mistrust?'

If she cleared the air, then maybe he would back
off. She didn't have to lie. She just had to be tact-
ful. He couldn't very well call her a downright liar,
could he? And if he was forced to tell her why he
was suspicious, then she might be able to fudge her
way through a few answers that might just satisfy
him. She wouldn't be here for ever. A few days of
peace was all she was after.

'I just can't picture the two of you together, as an
item,' Dante murmured softly.

Caitlin thought of the leggy Luisa and she stiffened at the implied insult.

'I suppose you think I should be more like that
ex-girlfriend of yours?' she said coldly. 'I suppose
that, because that's the sort of woman you like dating, it's only to be expected that Alejandro should

follow the same pattern? The last sort of woman he would ever go for would be someone like Luisa, even if, in *your* opinion, that would be the sort of woman you might be able to *picture* with him. As an item.'

Dante raised both eyebrows and there was a moment's silence.

'Are you insecure about the way you look?' he asked lazily, and if Caitlin could have gone any redder, she would have.

'Of course not!' She whipped her head away and stared out at the marvellous vista, not really seeing any of it but instead conjuring up an unflattering picture of herself alongside Luisa. She thought of the woman her ex-boyfriend had fallen for and hated herself for returning to that unfortunate place, which she'd thought she had left behind. She thought of all those leggy beauties next to whom she knew she often came up short in the eyes of the opposite sex. Tears gathered in the corners of her eyes and she took a deep breath, refusing to give in to the weak temptation to feel sorry for herself.

'Because you shouldn't be.' The words left Dante's mouth, a silky murmur that was as dangerous as a dark incoming tide. 'The likes of Luisa Sofia Moore can't hold a candle to you.'

He raked his fingers through his hair. He'd broken eye contact but he was still alive to her warmth, the feel of her next to him.

'It's not just about how you look,' he breathed, reluctantly turning back to her, ensnared by the pure crystal green of her eyes. 'So why is he with you? That's what I find so puzzling. You're not background, Caitlin. You might not stalk into a room like Luisa, but you still know how to make your voice heard. Nobody has ever talked to me the way you have. So, you and my brother, Alejandro, who has never been known to say boo to a goose? No. I'm just not getting it.'

Caitlin didn't say anything and, into the silence, Dante continued roughly.

'Me,' he breathed, 'I'm the sort of man who could handle you. Not my brother.'

Those words hung in the air between them and then he leaned forward and so did she, without even realising it.

Her body moved of its own volition. A fractional movement. Her eyes closed drowsily and there was a buzzing in her ears as his mouth hit hers, hard and hungry and demanding. His fingers curled into her hair and she didn't want to, knew she shouldn't, but she returned that devouring kiss as though her life depended on it and then, just like that, he was pulling back.

She looked at him, horrified.

'If I had any questions,' Dante said in a flat, hard voice, 'trust me, they have now been answered.'

With which he vaulted out of the water, his bronzed muscular body glimmering with droplets that glistened in the glare of the sun, while she remained frozen in place, like a block of ice.

Watching and barely breathing as he walked away.

CHAPTER SIX

DANTE DIDN'T KNOW who repelled him more. Himself, for his lack of control that had propelled him into crossing lines that should never have been crossed, or her, for crossing those lines with him when she was engaged to his brother.

He didn't glance back as he strode away from the pool back towards the house.

All those questions that had been buzzing in his head ever since he had found out who she was now raged inside him, an angry swarm searching for answers.

Work.

He would bury himself in his work because that always did the trick. He hadn't made it to the house before he realised that no amount of work was going to do the trick this time. He didn't know what Caitlin was doing. He didn't want to know. His mouth still burned from where her cool lips had opened beneath his and so, much to his rage, did his body.

He'd never responded to any woman the way he'd responded to her.

Was it because she was off limits? Maybe there was some deeply buried need to take what belonged to his brother. Was that it? Dante didn't think so. He had never wanted anything Alejandro had possessed. In fact he had no idea what women his brother had dated in the past, but he was quite sure he would never have dreamt of lusting after any of them. It just wasn't in his nature. He'd never lusted after any man's woman in his life before. Hadn't come close. He was a red-blooded male with a healthy libido and he enjoyed the pleasure of sex but, even in that faraway place where mistakes had been made, he couldn't recall having experienced this fury of attraction that wiped out everything in its path.

What the hell was going on here?

He dressed fast, shrugging out of his swimming trunks, replacing them with jeans and the first tee shirt that came to hand, and then back out he went, to his car, which was parked at an angle in the courtyard.

Where the hell was she? He hated himself for even wondering.

He arrived at the hospital with no idea where he was going with this, but he had a driving need to confront his brother, which was ridiculous given the fact that Alejandro was dead to the world.

Dante had kissed her. She'd kissed him right back. No coercion on his part! She'd melted in his arms and he had enjoyed every second of it. He just had to think about the piercing sweetness of her mouth,

the way her soft, small, luscious body had curved towards him, and he could feel the stirring of an erection. Her clear green eyes, as they had fastened on
him with smouldering hunger, had woken a sleeping
monster in him he hadn't known existed.

Dante was rarely confounded by anything or anyone, but he was confounded now.

The hospital was quiet as he made his way to his
brother's ward. They knew him at the desk so, when
he nodded at the little cluster of nurses and medics
chatting by the reception desk, they smiled and gave
him the go-ahead to enter the room.

He was going to have to tell Alejandro what had
happened. He was going to have to find answers to
the questions rolling around in his head. He was
going to have to try to find out what, exactly, was
going on.

He had no idea how he was going to accomplish
this because his brother wasn't going to be answer-
ing anything any time soon, but he had to get things
off his chest.

Dante pushed open the door and let it swing
on quiet hinges behind him, then he pulled one of
the visitor chairs next to the bed and looked at his
brother.

Now that everything had been stabilised, Alejandro could have been peacefully sleeping. His breathing was gentle and even.

'We need to talk,' Dante began.

He smiled at the incongruity of the statement,

then the smile disappeared and he thought, out of the blue, when had he ever said that to his brother? When had he ever met up with him just so that they could talk? About everything and nothing? Without a sense of duty hanging over both their heads, aware only that, as brothers, meeting up now and again, however uncomfortable, was just something they should do?

'Something has happened, Alejandro...' He structured his thoughts. Caitlin's image popped into his head, and he gritted his teeth together because never had his body been so relentlessly disobedient. How was he going to break this to his brother? Was it even right to try? He couldn't be sure that Alejandro would hear a word he said and, even if he did, who knew whether he would remember any of the conversation?

Many of Dante's doubts stemmed from his interaction with Caitlin. He had listened and watched and everything inside him had questioned the relationship she was purporting to have with Alejandro. Her reaction to Dante earlier by the pool...that kiss...was just the icing on the cake.

She wasn't some besotted lover, starry-eyed over his brother, counting down until the wedding bells began ringing.

Nor did his brother seem to be head over heels, like a swooning hero in a fairy tale.

But what if he was wrong about Alejandro? It wasn't as though he knew how his brother thought.

It wasn't as though they had the sort of bond that might allow him any insight into what went on in Alejandro's head and in his heart.

Was Dante willing to say what he had to say, to risk Alejandro taking everything in under that serene lack of consciousness and remember that the woman to whom he was engaged was not what she seemed?

Was Dante willing to break his brother's heart?

His jaw clenched. This sort of truth, he thought, was worth imparting. He wished to God someone had saved him months of pointless infatuation with a woman who had turned out to be as pure as mud, by setting him straight at the very outset.

Haltingly, expecting nothing in response, he began to explain.

Alejandro would sleep through it all. Dante was one hundred per cent certain on that point.

He was, however, wrong.

It took ages for Caitlin to get her act together because he had kissed her...no, they had *shared* that kiss... and everything inside her had gone into free fall.

She had felt his mouth on hers long after he'd disappeared back into the house and it was only when he'd gone that her brain had begun functioning and she'd remembered, with sickening horror, what he had flung at her when he'd walked off.

If he'd had any questions, then they'd been answered.

You didn't have to be a genius to get the drift.

She'd kissed him and the sham of her relationship with Alejandro had been revealed. In a handful of seconds, she had done the one thing she'd been determined not to do. She'd given the game away. Nor could she now be honest. How could she? Alejandro's secret was his to reveal, so she would have to accept that Dante would now see her as the worst possible candidate for the role of his brother's fiancée.

She hurried back to her bedroom, fearful that she might bump into Dante somewhere in the house, but she didn't. Just in case, however, she dressed quickly, and called a taxi to take her to the hospital. While she waited for it to arrive, she remained locked in her bedroom.

She had no idea what was going to happen next, but, playing it out roughly in her head, it involved her going to see Alejandro, where she would just have to explain what had happened and tell him, whether he could hear her or not, that she had no option but to return to London.

She could always leave a text on his mobile phone and he would pick it up as soon as he came to, and, naturally, she would phone the hospital daily, but leaving was her only option when the alternative was to run slap bang into Dante at some unspecified time in the future.

She felt very bad about his parents, but what choice did she have?

On the spur of the moment, she wrote a note, which she left in her bedroom, to be given to his mother, apologising for her abrupt departure and blaming work demands.

She would have some appreciation of what that meant considering at least one of her sons had sold his soul to the workplace.

The minute she thought of Dante, her mind began shutting down and her heart picked up pace and she had to close her eyes and breathe deeply so as not to feel faint.

That kiss.

There had never been anything like it in her life before. Jimmy…solid, reliable, steady Jimmy had never made her heart beat fast. She had liked him and they had fumbled around a bit but neither had had the slightest urge to take things to the ultimate conclusion.

He'd lived with his dad and she'd been living with her parents and it was a small village where everyone knew everyone else. Renting a room in their one and only hotel would have been ridiculous.

They would look forward to really enjoying making love when they were married, they had vaguely told one another. Actually, she wasn't even sure they had discussed it at all, simply assumed that that would be how things worked out between them.

Afterwards, when he had dumped her for the improbable model, she had been realistic enough to conclude that he hadn't pushed for sex because, as much as he'd liked her, he hadn't been attracted to her. Not really.

She hadn't stopped to ask herself whether *she'd* been attracted to *him*.

She'd nursed her wounded feelings and escaped.

Now, Dante had kissed her and it had been a thunderbolt. *That* was what passion felt like. *That* was the sort of aching and yearning that would have been impossible to ignore. She felt as though she had been sleepwalking and now she was fully awake, for better or for worse.

The taxi driver took his time getting to the hospital. On the way, he insisted on having a long conversation with her in Spanish, even though her responses were limited to an array of vaguely interested expressions and non-committal murmuring.

In her head, she was working out how she might get a flight back to London. Bye-bye to yet more money she didn't have. She would just have to go to the airport with her bag in hand, get to a ticket desk and pay whatever it cost for the first flight out.

Funny thing, she mused, hurrying into the hospital and pausing for a few seconds to get her bearings because the place was just so huge and she couldn't seem to keep a mental tab on which lift she needed to take to get to his ward, Alejandro would have understood her dilemma.

They would have spent hours laughing and talking about the mess she'd got herself into.

She hit the ward and was heading towards the reception desk when she saw Dante.

His face was grim, drawn. Given half a chance,

Caitlin would have fled in the opposite direction, but two things stopped her. The first was the sight of Dante striding towards her, a man on a mission, eyes firmly pinned on her hovering figure even though he was on his phone, talking urgently to someone at the other end.

The other was the fact that there was a commotion happening outside what seemed to be Alejandro's room, even though it was hard to be completely sure.

It was the latter that fired her forward and she reached Dante just as he shoved his phone back in his pocket.

'What's happening?' Caitlin breathed, trying to peer around his body but not getting very far. 'Is Alejandro okay? All those people… Is that his room or someone else's?' Her eyes were already filling up at the thought of her friend having some kind of unforeseen setback.

'My brother is awake.'

'What?'

'It is as if he's been having a nap and now he's up and ready to start the day.'

'That's…that's amazing. I have to go and see him, talk to him…' She took a step to the left and Dante reached out and blocked her from stepping forward with a hand on her arm.

Caitlin froze. Her mind emptied of everything. All she could feel was the burning touch of his fingers on bare skin.

'He's going to be wheeled off for a battery of

tests,' Dante was saying, while she desperately tried to focus on something, *anything*, other than his hand on her arm. 'There's no point in you trying to get to him.'

'But—'

'I've just been on the phone to my mother and said exactly the same thing to her. As you can imagine, she is as keen to see Alejandro as you are.'

Caitlin finally looked directly at Dante and inwardly quailed because all too clearly she could remember the inappropriate kiss that had galvanised his appalled withdrawal and damning judgement.

Should she bury the memory and pretend that nothing had happened between them? Or bring it out into the open, get rid of the elephant in the room before it started wreaking havoc? Or did it matter anyway, considering she was planning on clearing off as soon as she got back to Dante's house?

The decision was taken out of her hands when Dante said, coolly and firmly, leading her away from Alejandro's room towards the double doors back out into the main body of the hospital, 'You and I need to have a little chat.'

'About what?' At that very moment, Caitlin decided that pretending nothing had happened was definitely going to be the best option. 'I really think I should stick around here for a bit...see what's happening with Alejandro before I go—'

'Before you go?' Dante pulled to an abrupt halt and stared down at her with a veiled expression.

'Work is beginning to get a little impatient, Dante. I honestly can't stay over here indefinitely. My parents are also… They're anxious about me…'

'You're a big girl,' Dante gritted. 'I'm sure your parents will understand why you've stayed on.'

Caitlin didn't say anything. She had spoken to her mother the evening before and had detected the stress in her voice with a sinking heart. Her parents were clinging to their composure by the skin of their teeth and, more than ever in their lives, relying on her to steady them in stormy times.

Soothing, long-distance conversations were just not the same as seeing them face to face, being able to have a cup of tea, to hold her mother's hand and assure her that everything was going to be just fine.

Her father was doing his best, but he had always been the easy-going one between the two of them and now that her mother was on the verge of cracking up, her father was fighting his own battle with low-level panic, paralysed by the fear that everything he had worked for, what little remained, would somehow be wiped out from under his feet, and plagued with guilt at the thought that he had been the one responsible for all their problems.

How much longer could she just hang around?

'Don't tell me what my parents can or cannot understand,' she said sharply. 'I'm overjoyed that Alejandro has regained consciousness. I had planned on leaving later today but now I'll see him when he's up to visitors and I will leave for London as soon as I do afterwards.'

Dante didn't say anything. He had no intention of having any kind of showdown inside a hospital, so he spun round on his heels, making sure to keep his fingers firmly locked round her arm, and began leading her quickly towards the exit, ignoring the bank of lifts in favour of the stairs.

His car, in the underground car park, was waiting for them and they made their way there in complete silence.

There would be enough to talk about in due course, he thought.

'Where are we going?'

'To a café I know in the Plaza Mayor.'

'But can't you just tell me what you need to tell me right here?' She knew what he was going to say. He was going to mention that wretched kiss. He was going to voice all the suspicions that had been playing around in his head ever since he had set eyes on her. As far as he was concerned, she had offered up conclusive proof that he had been right to have been suspicious. He was going to call her to account and she couldn't blame him.

But it surely wasn't going to be a long conversation!

Was it even going to be a conversation at all? Or a full-frontal attack, which she would deal with by being as unresponsive as possible?

Judging from the way she had been frogmarched to his car, she was going for the full-frontal attack.

But at least they would not be having it at his house. At least, in the public arena, she wouldn't feel quite so overwhelmed.

And the Plaza was just a wonderful place, a beautiful rolling arcade ringed with stunning sepia- and pastel-coloured buildings, a tribute to history and the stunning architecture of the period.

She might just be able to sideline his attack by absorbing her surroundings, a sort of displacement therapy.

The café was nestled in one of the sepia-coloured shops. From the outside, it looked as though it might be on the verge of collapse. Inside, it was a marvel of modernity, with a long steel counter behind which five chic young girls catered for the needs of the most discerning of coffee drinkers and pastry consumers.

'I had no idea my brother would come to when I went to see him,' Dante opened. 'I had to go because of what happened between us at the pool.'

Caitlin cringed. 'About that…' she said faintly. She couldn't look at him. She couldn't meet those arresting dark eyes that were pinned to her face. For the first time, she wondered whether he had kissed her because he had been caught up in the moment, just as she had been, or whether he had kissed her as some kind of test to find out whether she really was the adoring fiancée she claimed to be.

She felt sick. Her stomach churned. All her insecurities pointed her in the direction of that kiss being nothing more to him than a means to an end. Why else would a guy like Dante, a guy who could turn his back on a woman who looked like Luisa, look at *her*? Yes, he had said something about her being *sexy*, but of course he would say that to butter her up and lower her defences for the moment when he leaned into her for that kiss, testing the ground, feeling his way to the answers he had been seeking.

'Yes?' Dante enquired coolly. He sat back as his double espresso was put in front of him, the attractive waitress taking her time as she positioned the cup *just so*. His eyes remained fixed on Caitlin's face, keenly noting the delicate bloom of colour in her cheeks. A guilty conscience would do that to a woman, he thought tightly.

'I never meant for that to happen.'

'I'm sure you didn't,' he responded smoothly. 'Engaged to one brother but happy to get into an intimate clinch with the other? Not exactly an example of a woman with sterling moral principles, is it?'

Trapped by a secret that wasn't hers to share, Caitlin could only bow her head in silence.

She would accept the full force of his condemnation. She would be gone in a heartbeat and she would be able to put it all behind her, except she knew that that would be easier said than done. Idiot that she was, she actually *cared* about what he thought of her.

Somehow, she had been incapable of locking the man away in a convenient one-dimensional box.

She'd tried, but he'd broken out of it and come right at her with all those complexities that had turned him into a living, breathing, fascinating guy who had fired her up in ways she would never have dreamt possible.

That was why she had kissed him. He stirred a crazy attraction inside her and she just hadn't been able to resist, but she knew how it looked on the outside. Kissing him had boxed her in as a two-timing woman who was happy to fool around behind her fiancé's back.

'You don't understand,' she said, without much hope of him paying a blind bit of notice to what she had to say. 'I know what it looks like, but I'm not that kind of person.'

'Thank you for telling me that. That answers all my questions.'

'There's no need to be sarcastic.'

'Then try coming at me with something a little better.'

'What do you want me to say?'

'What about the truth?'

'I'm telling you the truth. I'm not that kind of girl. I don't...' She looked away and fell silent because there was nowhere to go with an explanation.

'I told my brother about that kiss and you'll never guess his response.'

Caitlin was pretty sure she could.

'Actually, I had no idea my conversation would prove to be the thing that would rouse my brother

from his deep and peaceful sleep, but it was. I started
to talk to him...'

Dante paused and recalled the way he had felt,
opening up to a sleeping Alejandro. For the first
time he had felt something strong and bonding. It
had been the one and only meaningful conversation
he had ever had with Alejandro. The fact that Alejandro had been unconscious at the time had made
it easy, had removed the inhibitions born over time.

Dante met her eyes and sucked in a sharp breath.
So green, so crystal clear...so full of a disingenu-
ous innocence that was way off mark. 'I started to
talk to him and *bang*. He opened his eyes and was as
with it as though he'd never been dead to the world
at all. Funny thing, he didn't seem all that perturbed
by what we did. I had expected some kind of force-
ful reaction, had braced myself for his disgust and
loathing for my weakness. I didn't get any of that.
Does that surprise you?'

Faced with that direct question, Caitlin frantically
tried to compose an answer that would make sense.
The truth was off the table. She stared down at her
empty coffee cup and licked her lips nervously.

'He's...er...a very understanding kind of guy, as
I'm sure you'd know if you'd ever taken the time to
find out about him.'

Dante could only admire her attempt to divert him
from her non-answer by launching a missile at him.

'Nice try but it won't work.'

'Maybe we don't have a conventional relationship.' Caitlin didn't bother to ask him what he'd just meant by that because she knew.

'What do you mean?' Like a shark sensing blood, Dante felt on the verge of a revelation. If his head had temporarily been elsewhere, he was now once again committed to the task at hand. He pushed his cup to one side and leaned forward, resting his forearms on the table.

'I know what you were trying to do when you kissed me,' she said, swerving round his question.

'Come again?'

'You wanted to see if I would respond. You pretended to be attracted to me, you said lots of stuff you didn't mean, because you knew that if I responded then you would have all your suspicions confirmed. You want to push me into a corner and paint me black, but leading me on? That's sly.'

'You think I'm *sly*?'

Caitlin looked at him in stony silence.

'You couldn't be further from the truth,' he gritted brusquely. 'I'm not a man who plays that kind of game.' This was getting off point and he dragged his runaway thoughts back to the matter at hand.

'You and Alejandro. You were telling me that what you had wasn't a conventional relationship. Explain.' He shifted in the seat and tried to focus. He wasn't going to let her derail the conversation by veering off at random tangents, but he couldn't help but admire the antics. She was a match for him and he liked that.

'We were both great friends.' She was going to have to tiptoe round all manner of minefields, but Dante wasn't going to let up. 'Things went from there.'

Dante waited. Nothing further seemed forth-coming. He was very happy to play the long game, but eventually, he said, 'You *drifted* into a relation-ship because you happened to be good friends?' He looked at her with rampant incredulity.

'Friendship is a very good basis for a relationship,' Caitlin said defensively.

'And you would have married him? He would have married you? I find that hard to believe. For starters, you're young. Why would you abandon the one thing most women seem to want? Love, passion and a belief in fairy stories about happy-ever-afters? Nor do I understand why my brother would do the same.' But Dante knew that *he* had no faith in the institution of marriage. Love and fairy stories? No way. His own experience had taught him that any permanent relationship should always have a solid basis in reality. He'd fallen for the wrong woman once upon a time and his guard was permanently up. Maybe Alejandro was fashioned from the same cloth. Maybe he, too, had had an unfortunate experience that had taught him that a marriage of convenience was the way forward. Who knew?

And his parents *had* been getting quite vocal on the subject of their eldest son settling down.

Maybe he'd decided to opt for the friend knowing

that he wouldn't be troubled by a demanding or jealous woman who might end up wanting more than he was prepared to give.

That was certainly the lens through which he, Dante, viewed relationships...

He felt as though he was clutching at straws, but what else could explain his brother's nonchalant reaction to what had happened at the pool between himself and Caitlin?

But why would Caitlin have gone along?

'I had a terrible experience once upon a time,' Caitlin said softly, severing any further conclusions he might have been formulating on the subject of her and his brother. 'I was engaged to a guy. We'd known each other for ever, and in a small village like the one I grew up in that counts for something. Getting married was expected. Except no one—not me, not Jimmy, none of our family or friends—could foresee a five-foot-ten model swanning into his life and sweeping him off his feet.'

Reliving the moment, Caitlin realised that she felt next to nothing thinking about it now.

'He felt sorry for me. That was the toughest part. I suppose everyone did. I left for London and I put men behind me. I wasn't going to get involved with anyone ever again. Alejandro,' she tacked on truthfully, 'made sense.'

'Well, I hate to burst the bubble, but you might have to start rethinking that scenario,' Dante gritted. 'Alejandro's feathers weren't ruffled at the thought

of me kissing you. Are you happy to settle for someone who doesn't really give a damn what you do and
with whom?'

'I've talked enough,' Caitlin muttered, rising
to her feet. She felt hemmed in and suffocated by
Dante's oppressive presence and the sheer force of
his personality. 'I'm going to see Alejandro...'

'No point.' Dante stood up, dumping money on
the table, more than enough to cover the coffee they
had ordered. 'Like I said, he's having a battery of
tests. You won't be able to see him until tomorrow.'

'I'd planned on leaving this evening,' Caitlin reminded him, digging her heels in and refusing to
be bullied.

'That's the thing about plans. They often have
to change.'

For a moment, they stared at one another, and
then Caitlin broke eye contact and began walking
towards the door, only to stop because she was going
to have to return to the house and with Dante, unless he decided to hang around in the city centre for
no apparent reason.

'I'm very sorry about what happened at the pool,'
she said in a stilted voice as they began leaving the
city, heading out towards his house. *Clear the air*,
she thought. He had and so should she. 'I think it's
best if I pack my bags when I get back. Don't worry
about me. I've got stuff to do. Tomorrow, I can easily
take a taxi in to the hospital and then I can leave for
the airport straight from the hospital. I don't know

if I'll get a flight immediately but…but…' She ran out of steam and stared straight ahead at the scenery whipping past.

For a while, Dante didn't say anything.

He could sense her nerves. She had every right to be nervous. She also had every right to apologise about what had happened by the pool. He wasn't proud of himself, but he wasn't the one with a ring on his finger, even if the engagement was a complete sham from the sounds of it.

'I expect,' he said smoothly, 'that the touching engagement will now be a thing of the past? Our parents will be bitterly disappointed.'

Caitlin glanced at him.

This engagement was a charade but it was one that had suited both of them. So what happened next? It was something she would have to discuss with Alejandro. Did he still want to buy time? Dante might believe that theirs was just a convenient arrangement but many unions were based on less. She certainly wasn't going to commit to one thing or the other until she had spoken to Alejandro.

'Well?' Dante prompted sharply. They were nearing his house, all signs of habitation falling away to open land with the occasional manor to be glimpsed through imposing gates.

'I don't know what's going to happen.'

'You don't love my brother, Caitlin.'

'But I do.'

Dante killed the engine and swivelled so that he

was staring at her with brooding intensity. Frustration soared through him. He'd thought he'd got what he wanted but had he? What did she mean by that?

'Love without passion is the recipe for an empty marriage. And then there's us…let's not forget about that…' His voice was lazy now and pensive.

'There's no *us*.'

'No,' he agreed, 'there isn't, but you went up in flames when I kissed you. Don't worry. It was a mistake to touch you but I won't be succumbing to the temptation again. It's not in my nature to pursue any woman who belongs to someone else.'

Caitlin laughed shortly. '*Belongs to someone else?* What era are you living in, Dante? I don't belong to *anyone*.'

'Oh, but you do. Friends or no friends, you're my brother's lover—'

'I'm not!'

Stunned silence greeted this. For a moment, Dante was lost for words. The idea that two people could be engaged without having consummated their relationship beggared belief.

'And on the subject of lies…' Did she think he was born yesterday? Was she hoping to airbrush away their little moment of intimacy by pretending that fidelity to Alejandro wasn't imperative because they weren't lovers?

'I'm not lying,' Caitlin whispered.

'Tell me my brother isn't a substitute for your ex-lover,' Dante said sharply. 'No man wants to bed a woman who's thinking of some love she had and lost.'

'You don't get it, Dante!'

'*What* don't I get?'

'I'm not some scarlet woman! I haven't slept with your brother and…and…'

'And?'

'And I don't have any ex-lovers tucked away in my head, demanding my attention and messing up my life! I don't have any *ex-lovers* at all!'

'I don't get what you're saying.'

'What do you *not* get?' Caitlin finally snapped. 'I don't have any ex-lovers because I'm still a virgin!'

CHAPTER SEVEN

CAITLIN DIDN'T KNOW who was more stunned by that admission, Dante or herself.

She didn't wait to find out either, pulling open the car door and leaping out, heading at speed towards the front door.

Dante, on the other hand, took his time getting out of the car, grasping the roof and swinging his long body out.

Virgin? *Virgin?* Could she possibly be lying about that? No. He had seen the mortified embarrassment wash over her face in a red tidal rush, and he had known that she'd been telling the truth.

But her confession left him more confused than he already was.

Why was she engaged to his brother? What was going on? But then, the cogs in his brain began to crank back into life and he knew that there could be only one conclusion.

Alejandro was very kind, one of the world's gentle souls. Growing up, he had been the one in the kitchen helping the housekeeper cook while Dante had been kicking a ball outside or climbing a tree. Later, when rugby and black-run skiing had replaced the ball kicking, Alejandro had remained in the kitchen, but this time enjoying the business of preparing food and eating it, happy to read and pursue isolated hobbies. Dante had never really been able to get it.

What he was getting now, though, was the reality that his brother had doubtless found himself in a pickle. Their parents had become increasingly anxious to see their eldest son settle down and produce a few heirs to the throne.

And into this scenario, cue stage door to the left, came Caitlin, wounded by heartbreak, disillusioned with the whole business of love, and yet still desirous of having a family.

Two and two had made four and although she and his brother weren't in love, they liked each other well enough to do a sensible deal.

Hence Alejandro's lack of reaction when he, Dante, had mentioned that kiss by the pool.

He truly didn't fancy Caitlin. That was something Dante simply couldn't understand because he had never in his life found any woman more alluring.

A virgin!

He looked at her for a second, pausing. She was standing by the front door, every part of her body trembling with the urge to escape as fast as she could after her admission.

She couldn't have been dressed in an outfit less appealing to Dante. Somewhere along the line, she'd bought two long flowered skirts that harked right back to some distant hippie era. She was wearing one of these now. The mesh of swirling colours would give anyone a headache were they to make the mistake of staring for too long. Twinned with this was a short-sleeved tee shirt that was neither loose nor tight.

And yet nothing could disguise the intense sensuality of her body. He clenched his jaw hard.

Okay, so maybe the situation was a little more blurred than he'd first thought. Maybe what was an engagement, given the weird circumstances, couldn't be called *a relationship* at all. Doubtless it was just a matter of time before she broke it off, because all that rot about love and friendship counted for nothing when the shimmer of passion hovered in the background like a steady haze, and he had shown her that shimmer of passion.

Would she easily be able to go back to the empty dryness of a situation in which affection was the sum total of what she felt?

She was glaring at him, her face tight with the strain of suppressing her emotions, her hair all over the place. She looked like a wild cat and he marvelled that Alejandro could ever have thought that such a fiery creature could submit to a non-relationship indefinitely.

Heartbreak or no heartbreak.

Dante strolled towards her. She didn't have a key

or he was pretty sure she would have been firmly locked in her bedroom by now.

He slotted his key in the door, pushed it open and stood aside as she brushed past him.

'Caitlin.' His voice was rougher than he'd expected and he felt suddenly awkward.

'What?' She spun to look at him, her body taut and straight as an arrow, every nerve in her body still shimmering with heightened emotion. What had possessed her to share that most intimate of secrets with him? What?

'Join me in the kitchen for something to drink. Maybe eat. It's been quite a day.'

Caitlin opened her mouth to tell him that she would rather not but then she thought, so she had let slip that detail about herself... What of it? She had simply tried to defend herself against the slur of being a two-timer without a conscience. What was wrong with that? And what was the big deal with being a virgin? Why should she be embarrassed? It was her body to give when she wanted, not when the world deemed it suitable. She would far rather live a life being choosy about the person she chose to share herself with than sleep with any and everyone just because...

Besides, on a more pedestrian note, she didn't want to spend the remainder of the day hiding away in her bedroom. Why give Dante the satisfaction of thinking that he had got to her?

She could either allow herself to be swept along

on a fierce tide of helpless reaction or else try hard and fast to emulate his cool control.

She nodded and forced her reluctant legs to follow him into the kitchen.

Every gadget was high-end and polished to gleaming perfection, including the extraordinary coffee maker, which was a work of art in itself, but Dante bypassed that and headed for the fridge, which was concealed behind the banks of glossy grey cabinets.

It wasn't quite yet six but he offered her a drink, a glass of wine. Desperate to calm her nerves, Caitlin accepted with alacrity and finished glass number one at speed, instantly relaxing as the alcohol began coursing through her veins. It was easier to talk to Dante when she wasn't battling low-level panic and sickening awareness of his intense physicality. The wine lowered her defences and muted her nerves and, after a while, she knew that she was relaxing into normal conversation about Alejandro, now that he had regained consciousness, so she was unprepared when Dante suddenly sat forward, his dark eyes pinning her to the spot, his body angled forward so that she felt the heat he emanated.

'So talk to me. Tell me. I'm curious…' he said softly.

'Talk to you about what?' She had already finished two glasses of wine but as her eyes sought out the nearly empty bottle of Chablis, Dante relieved her of that easy route to Dutch courage by gently moving her glass out of reach.

'Why you've never slept with a guy.'

Instantly Caitlin stiffened. 'I should never have told you that.'

'But you did and I'm glad you did. The pieces are falling into place. So talk to me, Caitlin. Tell me why.'

'I already told you. I was hurt. I picked up the pieces and moved on.' She looked at him narrowly, alert for any show of mocking cynicism, but he was listening intently, his lean, beautiful face interested and non-judgemental, and she had a sudden fierce urge to confide. When she had left for London, she had locked away her past but now it was clamouring at the door, begging to be released. 'I just lost faith in relationships.' She paused. 'You wouldn't understand.'

'You might be surprised. I had a bad experience myself once upon a time.' Dante was shocked by an admission he had never shared with another living soul.

'Really?' Caitlin had never been more curious. 'Was it Luisa?'

That made Dante laugh, banking down his natural unease with sharing anything of a personal nature with anyone.

'I was nineteen,' he mused, 'and she was…older. With a child. I foolishly flung myself into something I thought had legs only to find out that she was not who she claimed to be. She was after my money and I had a lucky escape because I found out before I'd committed to something that would have ended up more than just a major headache. Nevertheless, I managed to squander a substantial amount of money in the process.'

Caitlin nodded, instantly understanding that, for a man as proud as he was, such a miscalculation would have been a source of bitter humiliation, even though he would never admit as much.

A low stirring began deep inside her. She felt hot and restless, her senses heightened in a way they never had been before in her life.

'But it wouldn't have occurred to me,' he continued, without breaking stride, 'to have given up on sex.'

'We're all different,' Caitlin said quietly.

'Know what I think?'

'I don't think I want to know what you think.' But she was frightened at just how much she really did.

'You know you do.' Dante tipped his finger under her chin so that she would focus on him and that simple gesture felt like something way more intimate, daringly intrusive even. Mesmerised, she could only stare at him. 'I think you're scared,' he said softly. 'I think my brother was the easy way out for you. Maybe you want a family and you can just about see your way to coupling with a man who couldn't possibly hurt you because you've handed nothing over to him, at least not the searing passion of real, complicated love. And perhaps my brother, who knows the weight of parental expectation, is prepared to buckle and accept what is on the table… Is that it?'

Caitlin said nothing. He had fumbled his way towards an explanation and, while he had hit the spot with certain assumptions, he was way off target with others, but then he was not to know the complexity of the situation.

One thing she was realising, though, was there was no way she could continue the pretence of an engagement to Alejandro, not to Dante or his family. He had forced her to recognise that passion was there; she had tasted it. The only problem was that the fruit she had tasted was forbidden. Dante was not the man for her.

'Stop asking me to talk about this,' she whispered.

'Are you really going to go ahead with a farcical engagement and a marriage that is going to eventually end in tears, whatever your reasons for instigating it?'

Caitlin could look at him now and say, truthfully, 'No.' She sighed. 'Are you satisfied?'

'Are *you*?'

'I need to go up now. I… I'm tired. I just want to have a long, hot bath and go to sleep.' She stood up because if she remained sitting, remained in his orbit, she knew that the urge to reach out and touch would be too powerful. 'I'm going to talk to Alejandro tomorrow and then…then… I'm going to head back to London…'

She talked to Alejandro. She'd thought that she might bump into Dante the following morning, and after the conversation they had shared she had been dreading that, but when, at a little after nine, she stepped into the taxi she had ordered to take her to the hospital, he was nowhere to be seen.

She wasn't sure what to expect but Alejandro was subdued, though very much with it and itching to leave the hospital. He was going to recuperate at his parents' house, he told her. The bones would heal and he would be on crutches within a week. Mobile. They got past the formalities of two people circling what they both knew was going to be the main event.

'I know you must have feelings for him.' Alejandro was the first to cross the Rubicon. 'You forget how well I know you. You need to be careful. He has a terrible reputation when it comes to women.'

'I'm not about to get involved with him, Alejandro.'

'But you'd like to?'

'No.' She'd thought of the way her body went up in flames whenever Dante was near her. She thought of those taboo images that had flashed through her head at regular intervals, hot and sharp and leaving her weak.

They'd spoken, Alejandro had said awkwardly. Dante had talked to him, openly and honestly, thinking him to be out of it. He had talked about how much he regretted the passing of time when they had had so little to do with one another. Caitlin could see that the Alejandro who had emerged from his deep sleep was a different Alejandro.

The engagement was no more. He would, he

told her, break it to his parents and hang the consequences. But he was still going to send her the money he'd agreed on, even though Caitlin was horrified and downright forbade it.

'I've already emailed my guy at the bank,' he warned her. 'A deal's a deal. Now, you go.' He smiled wryly. 'People are queuing to visit, including Luisa, for reasons best known to her. Can't remember her paying me a scrap of notice and I've known the woman since she was twelve.'

Something stirred in Caitlin. She remembered the venom on the other woman's face when she had bumped into them on the hospital ward not long ago, and shivered. Why would Luisa still be hanging around? Not her business. She was an old family friend. Did those ever really go away?

'That fall,' Alejandro's parting words were, 'might just have saved my life, Caitlin.' His voice was pensive. 'You should do what you feel you have to do. Take it from me, when you have a scare it makes you realise that life is precious and you only get to live it once…'

Her mind was on so many things when, much later, she let herself back into the house, having remembered this time to take a spare key. Two were kept in a metal safe in the kitchen and she had had to sign it out.

Having not seen Dante before she left for the hospital, she had taken it for granted that he would be similarly absent when she later returned.

He wasn't. Just as she was about to enter her bedroom to pack her bags to leave, he appeared at the opposite end of the corridor. Coincidence or not? Was he intending to continue his interrogation? Hadn't they both said enough? She desperately wanted a surge of inner strength to accompany those bracing thoughts, but it failed to materialise as he strolled towards her.

'How was he?' Dante asked quietly. He was holding his laptop under his arm, on his way to the important business of catching up on work, she thought. And it was pure coincidence that they had collided in the wide corridor. She could tell because he was in a rush, stopping only because politeness dictated that he did. That was the feeling she was getting. Their intimate conversation of the evening before had been buried for him. Maybe he felt that too much had been shared.

'Good,' Caitlin returned. 'I think he's going to get bored of being in hospital very soon. Apparently the broken bones are healing nicely. He'll be hobbling about before you know it. He's going to go stay with your parents and then, I guess, in due course, he'll return to London.'

'A single man...' Dante looked at her as her eyes shifted from his. He'd had time to think overnight. He couldn't remember a time when he had ever had as open a conversation with anyone as he had had with her and that, he had concluded, wasn't a good thing. Telling her...about that incident in his past had felt like a weakness, but it was too late to retrieve confidences shared and he wasn't going to waste time beating himself up about it.

He'd also had time to think about what she had told him about herself, her startling confession that she had never slept with anyone. She had been neither ashamed nor proud of her virginity. It was as it was, her attitude had implied and, while he admired her for that, he was in no doubt that she wasn't nearly as casual about her relationship status as she claimed to be.

She was so…fiery…so full of personality…so *opinionated*. How could she really be the sort to accept the reality of a relationship that delivered on all fronts except the single one that mattered, which was passion?

She might kid herself that she had squashed any romantic streak she might have had because of some broken heart back in the day, but she hadn't, and Dante had firmly made up his mind that, temptation or not, and whether she was now a free woman or not, he wasn't going to go there. Wasn't even going to think about it. She lacked the experience to deal with a sex-with-no-strings-attached situation.

Yet the delicate flush in her cheeks, the nerves she was trying hard to conceal, the intensely feminine *smell* of her…were all beginning to wreak havoc with his high-minded, well-intentioned resolutions.

'I'm keeping you. I was just about to pack my bags.'

'Pack?' That felt like a punch to the gut. Wrong reaction on every front.

'I told you, I intend to head back to London and the sooner, the better.'

That single sentence clarified everything in Dante's mind. It was one thing to be sensible when temptation wasn't staring you in the face. It was quite another when…it was.

She would leave and he wouldn't be seeing her again. He would be left wondering *what if…?* whether he liked it or not. The woman had got under his skin, and if she walked away now she would remain under his skin for ever. A burr he would not easily be able to yank free. An annoying itch that he would regret not having tried to scratch.

'Don't.'

That single word hung suspended in the air between them. Caitlin marvelled that a single one-syllable word could have such a dramatic effect on her senses. Her heart sped up. Her mouth went dry. Her pulses began to race.

'Yet. Don't leave yet.'

'What do you mean?'

'You know exactly what I mean.'

She did.

'There's no *you and Alejandro* any more,' Dante breathed thickly. 'Once upon a time, there was a convenient charade. That's over. You're a free woman.'

'It wouldn't work.'

'What wouldn't? Are you telling me that when you look at me...you don't want to touch?'

His voice had sunk to a husky murmur that felt like feathers brushing against her skin. She shivered. So many things were going round in her head right now, but top of the list was—*I want you... I don't know why, or how I could feel so attracted to you, but I want you...*

'That's not the point,' she responded, angry at the telltale weakness in her voice.

'Why?' All his natural aggression and instinct to pursue what he wanted surged to the surface, wiping out every mental obstacle in its path.

'How could a relationship work between us? Your parents...your friends...your relatives...all those people who had gathered there for the engagement party...what would they think?'

'Why would they know?'

'I don't understand.'

'I'm not talking about a relationship, Caitlin,' he husked. 'This would be sex. Pure and simple. I want you and you want me and one and one makes two. I'm not interested in getting involved with anyone with a view to anything other than having some fun. Yes, you have to get back to London, but you don't have to get back *just yet*.'

Every shred of heartfelt romanticism in Caitlin rebelled against the unadorned brashness of his proposition. There was no attempt to wrap it up as anything other than what it was—two people having sex for a few days before they parted ways, a ripple in both their lives, gone before it had had time to become anything bigger.

Caitlin was an unintentional virgin. She hadn't been saving herself for the right guy to come along. She hadn't slept with Jimmy for reasons that had become blindingly clear after he had fallen for the model, and since then she had retreated into herself. No one, not a single guy, had broken through the wall she had erected around herself. She'd pretty much come to the conclusion that she was frigid.

Sure, she wanted kids and a family and one day, she had vaguely thought, a guy would come along and she would be attracted to him and things would fall into place. It was a thought that barely registered on her radar, because she was just so busy building a career and, lately, stressing out about her parents. When it *had* registered, she had assumed the guy who eventually showed up would tick all the usual boxes. Nice, thoughtful, good sense of humour, non-smoker.

And yet here was Dante, all dark and dangerous, and definitely *not* Mr Nice and Thoughtful... And she wanted him so much it made her feel weak.

'I'm gathering from the prolonged silence,' he said wryly, interrupting the frantic racing of her thoughts, 'that sex without a *relationship* label attached to it isn't something you would be prepared to sample.' He lowered his eyes and her heart raced even faster.

'Although you'd be shocked at just how much fun it would be…'

He straightened. Somewhere along the line, they had moved close to the wall and he had been lounging against it, a long, lean, powerful jungle cat prepared to have a bit of fun with the antelope.

Antelopes, Caitlin thought in confusion, never came off well in any encounter with powerful jungle cats.

He was strolling away when all of a sudden she was galvanised into action.

He wanted fun. He wasn't relationship material and he hadn't bothered to hide that fact.

What was so wrong if she wanted a bit of fun, as well? There hadn't been much of that around for the past few months. She was here and she was only going to be here for a matter of a few days if she decided to stay on. After that, she would return to the reality of life on the other side of the ocean, back to the stress and the worry.

'Dante!' Crunch moment. She took a deep breath and was suddenly filled with a wave of pure, fizzing excitement.

He'd stopped, turned round and was looking at her with lazy interest.

He hadn't expected her to stop him but now that she had, he was aware of a soaring sense of relief. He hadn't realised just how much it had meant for her to come to him, and not because he had kissed her or tried to seduce. He hadn't wanted her to be swept away in the moment. He'd wanted her to make a conscious decision in the cold light of day.

He looked at the sexy sashay of her rounded hips and banked down the fierce ache of an erection.

'Yes.' Caitlin cleared her throat and looked at him without flinching.

Dante didn't say anything for a couple of seconds, then he reached out and cupped the side of her face, his long fingers soft and tender, stroking the satin smoothness of her cheek.

When he kissed her, she finally discovered what it felt like for the earth to stop spinning.

CHAPTER EIGHT

THEY MADE IT to his bedroom, fingers entwined. He nudged the door, which was slightly ajar, with his foot and, instead of turning on the overhead light, he just wrapped his arms around her in the gathering darkness in the bedroom and held her close.

'Would you listen to me if I told you not to be nervous?'

It was the one thing guaranteed to calm her nerves and it did. She visibly relaxed and settled into the embrace, her head resting on his chest so that she could hear the faint beating of his heart.

She tentatively wrapped her arms around him, then slid them underneath the polo shirt and shivered at the feel of muscle and sinew under her fingers. Very gently, he mimicked what she was doing. Without making a big deal of it, he expertly unclasped her bra.

Caitlin gave a soft whimper as he curved his big hands under her breasts, stroking the crease beneath them and then, very slowly, working his way up until he was massaging both her breasts, and as he massaged them he rubbed the pads of his thumbs over her stiffened nipples.

'You have no idea how long I've wanted to do this,' he murmured. 'I'm hard like steel for you. One touch and I don't know what the outcome will be. I might embarrass myself by not being able to hold back... If I make you nervous then, rest assured, you make me nervous, as well...' He wasn't kidding. The gentle, shyly faltering sweep of her hands along his body made him wonder whether he would be able to last long enough to actually get inside her.

'No, I don't,' Caitlin breathed. She was hopelessly drifting on a current of such pure, delicious sensation. Her nipples were tingling and, between her legs, her panties were wet. Her clothes felt like an impediment. It was as if, slowly but surely and without attempting to remove a single article of clothing, he was somehow managing to get her to a place where she wanted to rip them all off.

Dante laughed softly. He looked down at her upturned face and lowered his head to kiss her. It was a long, leisurely, lingering kiss, and he didn't stop touching her nipples, playing with them, teasing them so that she was squirming, her whole body hot and restless.

He made no attempt to touch her anywhere else. Just that kiss that went on for ever and the light, lazy caress of her breasts. It was driving her crazy.

She broke free and began tugging him towards

the bed. She could hear her own breathing and then a low laugh from him.

'I'm taking my time,' he husked.

'You're driving me nuts,' Caitlin responded with staccato jerkiness, and he laughed again.

Through the window, the declining sun was casting long shadows into the bedroom. The open shutters turned the light into stripes. It was still very warm outside, but here in the bedroom it was beautifully cool. Thick walls, she assumed. A fortress of a mansion that could withstand the heat of summer and the cold of winter.

She was pulling him towards the bed and when she felt the side of the mattress against her knees, she sank down and then looked up at him. He was standing over her and, very, very slowly, he began to undress.

Nervous? No way could this man ever be nervous when it came to making love but, she thought, he'd been kind to have said so because he'd have known that she would have found it endearing and a little funny and it would have relaxed her even more.

Everything he was now doing spoke of self-assurance and complete confidence in himself.

Of course, she'd seen him in his swimming trunks, but it was different now because, this time, this was going somewhere. She was appreciating the broad, naked chest and the muscled width of his shoulders in an entirely different way.

He flung the polo shirt on the ground and then

his hand hovered for a few seconds on the zipper of his trousers.

Caitlin's breath hitched in her throat.

'You're so perfect,' she breathed, and he burst out laughing.

'And you're so honest. I like that.' He stepped out of the trousers but kept the boxers on. 'You don't play games in bed. It's refreshing.'

She could see the bulge of his erection and it made her feel faint.

She was sitting on the side of the bed and he nudged her legs open so that he was standing between them.

'I want to see you.'

With a few words, her excitement was ratcheted up a few notches and she hooked her fingers under the baggy tee shirt and pulled it over her head, taking the bra with it at the same time.

Her instinct was to cover her nakedness with her hands, but Dante was far too expert a lover to allow her to hang on to her natural reserve and, with a few adept touches, she shed her nervous apprehension and began to relax.

Dante stared. He couldn't help himself. He'd seen some of the most beautiful women on the planet and yet this one…got to him in all sorts of places no one else ever had. That was a mystery to him, but then the circumstances were completely different from any he'd ever been in before and, beyond that, he had shared more of himself with her than with any other woman. Another mystery.

Her breasts were full, more than a handful and tipped with perfect pale brown discs, large and succulent and inviting.

He stifled a groan and reminded himself that he had to go slow. It was going to be a feat of willpower.

He lowered himself, boxers still in place, and knelt between her, urging her to sit up so that he could suckle her breasts one at a time.

Caitlin arched back, eyes shut, rocked to the very core. She curled her fingers into his dark hair. She needed to get rid of the rest of her clothes. When she'd walked towards him in the corridor, when she'd made that momentous decision to sleep with him, she'd braced herself for all the nerves she'd known would accompany her first time making love, but her nerves had disappeared, overridden by fierce, burning *need*. It cut through everything.

He pushed his hand under her skirt and skimmed her thighs. Her skin was satiny soft and smooth. He nudged his knuckles against her crotch and felt her dampness. For a second, he had to empty his head because the whole situation was far too erotic, from her soft moans to the pliancy of her sexy body. She was giving him the gift of her virginity and for a moment he was filled with doubt, then he wiped that clean from his head because they were both adults and choices had been made, eyes wide open.

And in a way, wasn't he doing her a favour? As

time went on, her virginity would surely become an albatross round her neck, a prize to be given to Mr Right, except would there ever be a Mr Right? Did that person exist? Or would she end up trusting some guy like her ex, only to be let down? Wouldn't her heartache be a thousand times worse because she would have opened herself up to that person, expecting all the fairy stories peddled by the rest of the world? At least, with him, he wasn't selling her stories or making promises he couldn't keep. Theirs was a straightforward arrangement.

Dante pushed the skirt up and she wriggled so that it was ruched and gathered at her waist. It felt wildly decadent. He was still there, between her legs, and modesty slammed into her when he inserted his finger underneath the stretchy fabric of her underwear, but he gently eased her hand away.

He linked his fingers through hers and kept her hands still at her sides, then he nuzzled against the damp underwear, breathing in her musky smell. He tasted her through the silky barrier. He was going to go further, going to feel her wetness on his face, but not yet.

The need to be gentle, to take his time, to make sure she enjoyed this first experience felt crucially important. She never hesitated when it came to speaking her mind, and she'd had more to say on the subject of him and his lifestyle than anyone else in living memory, but, emotionally, he sensed a curious vulnerability and that vulnerability, now, was bringing out in him a protective streak he hadn't known he had.

He unclasped their hands and waited until he knew that she was ready, then he eased the underwear off and parted her legs.

No underwear now as a barrier and the honeyed sweetness between her thighs was a powerful aphrodisiac. Dante licked and sucked. Easily finding the throbbing nub of her clitoris, he began to tease it until she was writhing with mounting pleasure.

His own erection was a steady, pulsing ache in his groin. No problem. The second he entered her, he knew that he was going to come very quickly. For the moment, he would devote all his attention to getting her to that place where she was desperate for him to sink into her.

He continued to feast on her wetness until her cries became more demanding.

'Please... Dante...' Caitlin said brokenly. 'I'm going to... I won't be able to help myself...' She didn't want to come against his mouth. She wanted to feel the closeness of him inside her.

Never in her wildest dreams had she ever imagined that sex could be this good.

When he stood up, it left a cool void, and in the ever-darkening room she followed his progress to the dressing table, where he found his wallet and very quickly spun round, ripping off the tin-foil wrapping of a condom.

Protection. Of course. And in his wallet. A man who was not prepared to take chances.

She sat up and pulled down the skirt just as he did the same with his boxers. She gave a sharp intake of breath and a prosaic thought flitted through her head... *Will he fit inside me?*

He was impressively big. She watched as he walked slowly towards her. His eyes were pinned to hers but he was absent-mindedly holding himself with his hand. Watching as he stroked himself was an incredible turn-on.

Her eyelids fluttered. She shuffled into a horizontal position, barely able to keep any part of her body still, busily drinking in the truly beautiful sight of his nudity. Where she was milky white, he was so sexily bronzed, and when he joined her on the bed she could only marvel at the difference in colour between them.

He manoeuvred her so that they were facing one another and ran his hand along her side, enjoying the dip of her womanly waist and the flare of her hips.

It was incredibly intimate looking deep into his eyes from this close.

'Are you relaxed?'

'I wasn't to start with.'

Dante half nodded and smiled. He slipped his hand between her legs and cupped her. He didn't go any further than that. He just cupped her there and moved his hand until she wanted so much more, until she was quivering, her fingers digging into his shoulders and only then, when he had roused her to fever pitch, did he move over her and gently begin to insert himself.

He felt her nerves, the way she stiffened, and he began whispering into her ear, soothing her as he eased himself in.

She was so wonderfully tight, scared and nervous now but, oh, so eager for him.

Dante had to grit his teeth not to push hard and satisfy himself. Bit by bit he entered her, her wetness easing a path, her groans escalating in volume the deeper he was and when, at last, he had that final thrust, Caitlin was ready for him and her body responded with enthusiasm. He moved and she moved as well, their bodies in total harmony.

It felt so good. Unbelievably so. Dante came with an explosion that shocked him in its intensity.

Her own orgasm followed his. She arched up to him and cried out, all inhibitions gone in that moment.

Afterwards, it was like swimming back up to the surface having been underwater. Caitlin sighed and shifted so that they were belly to belly. Never had she felt closer to anyone and yet, even as she knew that, she also knew that that was an admission she should never make.

'That was the best,' she said with honesty. 'At least,' she added, even more honestly, 'for me. I don't suppose it was much of a deal for you.'

'Don't even think of saying something like that.' Dante kissed the side of her mouth and ran his fingers through her tangle of colourful hair.

Dante had become jaded over time. In business, he got what he wanted. He was single-minded, focused, ambitious and feared. Born into wealth, he had continued climbing up that ladder, unimpeded. The sense of satisfaction he had felt when he had first started diversifying and doing his own thing, setting up his own empire, had become a dull, background acceptance of success. Winning deals, absorbing companies, the thrill of being the first to spot the gold mine waiting in the wings...the shine had worn off. Thinking about his brother and his dislike of the job he had inherited, his forays into other worlds that had nothing to do with money but were adventures to be had and nothing more, Dante felt a sharp pang of envy.

He was the younger but a lot more cynical.

And when it came to women...

Dante gazed at the woman lying next to him, warm and drowsy post-sex.

He would tire of her. He always did. He wondered whether his defence mechanisms against becoming too involved with any woman were so finely honed that it made it impossible for him to have anything approaching a normal relationship. No sooner had he slept with a woman than his attention began to stray. It was something he had long accepted. It was why he found the idea of marriage so inconceivable and why, if it ever hovered at the back of his mind, it was in the shape of something convenient, without the exhausting, futile and complicated shenanigans associated with emotion.

'Penny for your thoughts,' Caitlin said lightly, her clear green eyes not shying away from him.

She had her life to get on with. He had his. She would find someone eventually and her belief in love would be rekindled.

'You could stay awhile,' he murmured.

Caitlin looked at him seriously. 'I have a job to go back to.'

'Jobs can wait.'

'That's fine for you to say. You're your own boss and you can afford to do what you want.'

But that invitation was so tempting, even though she could read the corollary... *Stay awhile because pretty soon I'll get fed up anyway...*

'Don't you want to...to do this all over again?'

She hesitated, and in that pause he smiled slowly.

'Because I really want to.'

'I have responsibilities.'

'I'm not talking about a long-term arrangement, Caitlin. I'm talking about a few days of uncomplicated fun before we go our separate ways.' He stroked her side and her eyelids fluttered. 'Your responsibilities will be waiting for you when you get back to London, I'm sure.'

They would, Caitlin thought. Her parents...the stress...the uncertainty...none of that would be going anywhere any time soon. Alejandro had told her that he had instructed his bank to deposit the promised money into her account. She had no intention of keeping any of it so she would be back to square one when she returned to London.

But was she really the sort of person who could enjoy a few days of guilt-free pleasure without consequences? She'd shrugged off the whole business of relationships but, looking back at it, she hadn't been tempted into any anyway, so shrugging them off hadn't been an issue.

But she and Dante had slept together.

Lust.

That was what it had all been about. Lust and maybe the allure of being in a different country, where grim day-to-day reality could be kept at a distance... It was as real as stardust.

He wanted days. She could do days. Lust faded. And what was wrong with snatching a little time out?

His parents wouldn't know. Alejandro would probably suspect but he would be amused. They would live in a little bubble for a week and then the bubble would burst and that would be that. No harm done.

'Okay.' She blushed. She reached out and did what he was doing to her: she stroked him, her fingers sliding over taut sinew and muscle, then lower to where his stirring erection left her in no doubt that what he felt for her was very, very genuine. 'You're right. Responsibilities can wait awhile...'

His parents wouldn't know. They would be spared the bewilderment of thinking that she had been engaged to one brother only to move on to the next. Without the complexities of the situation being explained, how could they think otherwise? They lived some distance away so it wouldn't be an issue. Somehow, Caitlin had managed to avoid another dinner invitation and she suspected that that was because they were too wrapped up with events to even think about entertaining their son's fiancée, however much they might have wanted to.

Dante, perhaps, had engineered things so that they could have time to themselves, in that very special bubble where the past and the future didn't exist, just a very physical and very exciting present.

'It's extraordinary,' he had told her the evening before, when they had lain together, their limbs entangled so that they were almost a single unit, 'but this is the best sex I've ever had.'

Caitlin had laughed and quelled the unexpected hurt she had felt. *The best sex*... Maybe there were women who would have seen that as a compliment. She could understand that. Dante was a man of experience, a man who could have any woman he wanted at the snap of an imperious finger, so doubtless when he'd said that, it had been said as a compliment.

But for Caitlin...since when had that ever been her dream? Since when had she ever thought that she would end up snatching time with a guy who wasn't interested in anything beyond a romp in the sack? Had she ever thought that she would be helplessly sucked into the sort of non-relationship she had been schooled to avoid at all costs?

And yet, those words had filled her with a guilty pleasure.

She had to keep reminding herself that none of that really mattered because she would soon be gone.

Alejandro would soon be leaving hospital. She had visited him first thing this morning and he had been upbeat. He had shrewdly asked her about Dante and she had not committed to any kind of answer, but he had gone ahead and warned her off him again anyway, as if she had needed that warning.

Right now, Dante would be on his way back from the hospital. He had gone to work—an urgent meeting, he'd said, but he would much rather have lazed in bed with her—and would be stopping on the way back to his house.

Caitlin had already been there for an extra three days. Mentally, she had dealt with extending her stay by a week. That gave her four more days to bask in their short-lived relationship. When she thought about boarding that plane back to London, her mind skittered away from the unpleasant feeling that that was the last thing she wanted to do and, she told herself sternly, that had nothing to do with the fact that she hated the thought of never seeing Dante again. It was simply because she was having a holiday from all her stress and who ever wanted a holiday to come to an end? No one.

Standing in the kitchen now, with a bottle of wine

chilling in the fridge and a meal in the oven, prepared by one of the three members of staff permanently employed to make sure that no need of Dante's ever went untended, including the need to eat extremely fine food and drink extremely fine wine, Caitlin glanced down at her outfit.

She had forgone the usual uniform of loose skirt and loose top, which Dante referred to as her *hippie chick outfits*, and was wearing a pair of skinny jeans and a fitted top, which she had bought the day before. Huge extravagance and she had no idea why she had done that, except she'd been out with Dante and he had practically shoved her into the shop and then had declared the outfit an amazing fit when she had grudgingly paraded it for him. She'd been squirrelling every spare penny into an account for her parents and hadn't spent anything on herself for ages and suddenly, for no reason, she'd felt reckless.

Regrettable, considering her arrangement with Alejandro had bitten the dust, even though, up to this morning, he'd pressed her to take the money, which he didn't need and she desperately did, and not be silly. He'd refused to give her his bank details. She would sort that out as soon as he was out of hospital, she'd decided.

And she had to agree with Dante—the outfit suited her.

An uneasy thought surfaced. Was she, subconsciously, dressing to please him because she wanted to somehow persuade him into a relationship he had declared he didn't want? Did she want a week to stretch into a month? A year? Longer?

If that were the case, which she wasn't even going to give houseroom in her head, then she had obviously lost her mind.

She didn't hear him enter.

She'd been lost in her thoughts. Then she looked up and there he was and her heart skipped several beats.

He was so breathtakingly beautiful, so spectacular in every possible way, that she could only stare and blink for a few seconds, like a rabbit caught in the headlights. He was magnificent naked but no less so when he was kitted out in his handmade leather shoes and the designer suit that would have cost the earth.

He'd dumped his jacket somewhere along the way and unbuttoned the top three buttons of his white shirt, which was cuffed to the elbows. His trousers, pale grey and hand-tailored, were a beautiful fit and somehow managed to make him look businesslike yet crazily sexy. Quite an achievement, she thought faintly.

Eventually, their eyes met and she blinked.

'What's wrong?' How quickly she had become used to his eyes darkening when they rested on her, to the slow, unfurling smile that could make her toes curl and bring a surge of heated colour to her face.

Right now, as he remained standing by the kitchen door, his face was grave and that sent a chill of foreboding through her.

'We need to talk.' Dante didn't take his eyes off her as he walked directly to the fridge to pour them both a generous glass of Rioja.

'You think I might need a drink to cope with whatever you have to say?'

He'd moved to sit at the table and she followed suit, although adjacent to him with a chair between them. Close enough to lean into whatever conversation was about to take place but far enough for her to remove herself from the suffocating effect he had on her senses.

She tried to read what he was thinking but he was adept at concealing what he wanted hidden.

'It's about my brother.'

'But...' she half rose '...I was with him this morning and he was absolutely fine.'

Dante tilted his head to one side. 'He told me.'

'He told you...?'

'Caitlin...you should have said. No, scratch that... of course, you couldn't have broken the promise you made him but...' Dante rubbed his eyes wearily. 'I wish I had known.'

'Alejandro *told* you?' Shocked, Caitlin leaned towards Dante, her urgent green eyes colliding with his weary dark ones. He looked drained. More than that...he looked *saddened*.

She reached out and covered his hand with hers and breathed a sigh of relief when he curled his fingers into hers. He slumped back in the chair for a few seconds, eyes closed, then he opened his eyes and looked at her.

'We spent years growing more and more distant from one another. I had no idea how he felt about working for the company until you told me. I had no inkling that he was gay and the worst of it was that he felt so damned apprehensive about telling me. Yet he had every right to keep it to himself. When have I ever given Alejandro any indication that I was interested in his personal life? We were ships that crossed in the night, exchanging as little as possible of any significance.'

'That's sometimes how it goes,' Caitlin told him gently. 'But there is an opportunity now for things to change between you. He's your brother and you're so lucky to have a sibling.' She thought of the cares and troubles she was having to manage single-handedly. 'Alejandro is one of the kindest people I've ever met and I know he would be so happy, so thrilled and excited, to have you in his life. I mean, properly in his life.' She paused. 'Has he...er...broken this news to anyone else?'

'He's going to tell our parents later today. He's wary, he tells me, but it's something he said he should have done a long time ago. I think coming here under those false pretences, his fall...brought home to him the need to come out and be honest.'

'I'm really glad he has,' Caitlin admitted. 'You have no idea how hard I've tried to persuade him that living a lie wasn't a good idea.'

'You agreed to the charade,' Dante mused softly, 'because he was so desperate to do what he thought he needed to do, didn't you? He talked you into pretending to be his fiancée and you agreed because that's just the kind of person you are…'

Uncomfortable with this summary of events, Caitlin shuffled in the chair and wondered whether she should launch into the full account of the harebrained scheme they had agreed upon.

She remained silent. What would be the point? The main thing was that all the hiding behind closed doors was over for Alejandro and a new chapter in his life was about to begin.

'Yes, I'm a saint,' she quipped. 'If you'll excuse me, I'll just vanish upstairs for a minute so that I can polish my halo.'

Dante burst out laughing. His eyes darkened with appreciation.

There was something *special* about her. The fact that she had stepped up to the plate and done something as dramatic as she had, for the sake of friendship, struck him as almost noble.

Would she have carried on with the pretence? And for how long? Yes, she had been hurt in the past, but would that hurt have propelled her into a permanent arrangement with Alejandro if events had not played out the way they had?

He also admired the fact that she could have told him. She could have broken that confidence, knowing that it would have put a completely different slant on things. She must have known, after that kiss they had shared at the pool, that his opinion of her would have been in the dirt when he'd walked away. But she hadn't followed him. She had remained true to the promise she had made his brother.

Self-serving she was not, and he really liked that.

And now...

Dante had truly thought that her novelty value would have worn off by now. Here they were, playing truant from reality like a couple of heady teenagers, and he had assumed that the sheer *difference* about her, the very thing he figured had got to him in the first place, would have worn thin by now.

Yet he saw her and he wanted her. He touched her and he had to stop himself from shaking. He heard that infectious laugh and he smiled.

And now everything had changed and a forbidden thought crept into his head like a thief in the dark.

What if they carried on for longer than the week prescribed? He wasn't looking for permanence and neither was she. He'd half feared that she might have begun to view what they had as more significant than he had told her it was destined to be, but there had been no hesitant forays into a future beyond the coming weekend. She had not hinted at wanting any more than what they had agreed upon. She had been as casual as him, living in the moment and enjoying it.

'I like your sense of humour,' Dante confessed, his thoughts still running unchecked. 'Women have always been way too eager to do what they think I might like. You're not like that…'

'You live in a different world, Dante.' But Caitlin was inordinately pleased by the compliment. 'I guess people suck up to you because of who you are and you've become accustomed to that. I don't live in that world and it's not how I've been brought up.' She smiled. 'We're all different.'

'And I like that. More than I thought I would.'

'What do you mean?'

'Things have changed with Alejandro's revelation. My parents, for better or worse, will find out that the engagement they had such high hopes for was all a pretence. Well intentioned, but still a pretence. Alejandro is terrified that they will pass judgement and he will be found wanting. I like to think that that is not going to be the case. At any rate…' he looked at her, his lean, handsome features decisive '…you will be able to face them for who you really are.'

'I won't be facing them, Dante,' Caitlin said with alarm. 'I'm leaving in a few days. There's really no need for me to meet up with them again.'

Still accepting of her departure, Dante thought with appreciation. Not going beyond the brief. A first. He was accustomed to having his freedom threatened sooner or later by women who wanted more longevity than he was prepared to give.

He shrugged and smiled. 'You can go at the end of the week,' he concurred, 'or you can stay on. Better still, I can arrange to temporarily transfer to London, sort things out in my brother's absence...'

'You want to *carry on*?'

'For a while,' Dante said hurriedly.

He isn't bored yet, Caitlin thought. *But soon he will be.*

He wanted everything on his terms, but what about hers? She was in danger of forgetting them, and she couldn't afford to do that because every day something deep inside was being chipped away.

'I don't think so.' She didn't wait for temptation to start interfering with common sense. 'Let's have fun and then, at the end of the week, let's do what we agreed to do. Let's say goodbye.'

CHAPTER NINE

IT WASN'T DIFFICULT to find out where Caitlin lived. Far more difficult had been Dante's decision to travel to London and search her out, because it just wasn't in his nature to pursue anyone. Pursuit equated to weakness, but, after more than two weeks without her, Dante had managed to convince himself that the real weakness would be in staying put, in ignoring the perfectly reasonable desire to finish something that had not quite reached its natural conclusion. How could he live with himself if he remained where he was, pointlessly thinking about her and having nightly cold showers? Did that make any sense at all? If she turned him away, then so be it. He would shrug it off but at least he would have tried, and you couldn't do more than that. The not trying would have been the less courageous option.

As promised, she had remained in Spain for the remainder of the week, daily visiting Alejandro, who, having awakened from his deep sleep bright-eyed and bushy-tailed, had been frustrated at not being able to get out of hospital as fast as he had hoped, thanks to the small detail of broken bones that needed to rest awhile.

Part of his urgency to leave had been sheer relief at having come out. He had told the world and the world had been a lot more forgiving than he had anticipated.

What his traditional and old-fashioned parents had made of the whole thing was a mystery to Dante. Outwardly, at least, they had been supportive and that had been the main thing.

And now that barriers had broken down between himself and his brother, they had begun the rocky but well-intentioned road of making amends for the silent relationship that had developed between them over the years.

Between building bridges with Alejandro, engaging with his parents and all those family members now on the receiving end of what would have been, at the very least, pretty startling revelations, and focusing on some major deals in the pipeline, he should have found Caitlin's easy disappearance from his life barely left a ripple in its wake.

It had been a source of constant frustration that he couldn't get her out of his head. He had been forced to conclude that it hadn't been just about the sex. He had enjoyed her company and he didn't much like that recognition, because it wasn't something he had factored into their short-lived relationship.

So here he was.

He could have asked Alejandro for her address,

but he knew, instinctively, that his brother would have cautioned him against prolonging a relationship with someone he obviously cared about. Deep and meaningful conversations he and Alejandro might not have had, but that didn't mean that Alejandro was ignorant of Dante's womanising lifestyle choices. He wouldn't have understood that he and Caitlin were on the same page when it came to their relationship. She wasn't going to lose her head over him. She wasn't going to get hurt. Why else would she have found it so easy to walk away? There hadn't been so much as a hint that she'd been looking for more than what had been put on the table.

He'd asked his PA to get hold of her address and, lo and behold, it had taken under half an hour.

He hadn't known what to expect of her living arrangements and was shocked to discover himself standing, now, outside something that looked as though an act of kindness would have been to take a wrecking ball to it. But then, he acknowledged grimly, his background had not prepared him for the reality of living on the breadline.

It was a squat, rectangular block of flats, all connected by outside concrete walkways. Washing lines groaning under the weight of clothes only partially concealed chipping paint. Bikes were leaning in front of most of the flats. The lighting was poor and Dante concluded that that was probably a good thing, because in the unforgiving light of day the sight would probably be twice as depressing. He had never been anywhere like this in his life before and he was shocked and alarmed that she lived in a place like this.

Was she going to be in?

He'd taken a chance. It was after nine on a Wednesday evening. He was playing the odds.

He took the steps two at a time. There was a pervasive odour in the stairwell but he didn't dwell on that as he headed up to the third floor, then along the walkway, brushing past the washing, dodging the bikes and random kids' toys and finally banging on her front door because there was no bell.

And then, suddenly nervous, Dante stepped back and waited to see what would happen.

Caitlin heard the banging on the door and assumed it was Shirley three doors down. She had a good relationship with the much older woman. Too good, in some ways, because Shirley was a lonely seventysomething and, for her, Caitlin was the daughter she'd had but who now never visited.

Caitlin slipped on her bedroom slippers, pulled open the door and then stared.

The whole hit her before the detail. She knew it was Dante. Half lounging against the wall, hand poised to bang once again on the door. Yes, she registered that, then she absorbed, numbly, the detail. The faded black jeans, the grey polo shirt, the weathered bomber jacket because summer was morphing into autumn and the nights were getting cooler.

'What are you doing here?' she asked faintly, hovering by the door, so shocked that she could barely think straight.

She'd been thinking about him and he'd materialised like a genie from a lamp, as beautiful and as cruelly mesmerising as she'd remembered. She'd stayed those last few days and stuck fast to her insouciant *this-is-fun-but-it's-got-to-end* routine, but every second had been filled with the wrenching pain of knowing that she would never see him again, and since she'd returned to London the pain had not subsided. He'd filled her head every waking moment, obliterating everything, even the ongoing anxiety about her parents. And now, shockingly, here he was. They'd had a straightforward deal and she'd spent the past weeks reminding herself of that baldly unappetising fact, but now he was here and she felt the electric buzz of awareness zip through her body like a toxin.

Dante lowered his eyes, his long, dark lashes brushing his slanting cheekbones and shielding his expression.

The nerves had gone. She was standing in front of him and the nerves had been replaced by a racing excitement. She was in some loose, hanging-around, *who-cares-how-I-look?* clothes. Baggy jogging bottoms, baggy sweatshirt, weird fluffy slippers. Her hair was loose, a riot of vibrant curls spilling over her shoulders and down her narrow back.

He'd never seen anything quite so beautiful in his life before.

She'd asked him a question. What was it? His breathing had slowed and when he raised his eyes to meet hers, it was like being hit by a sledgehammer.

He said the one and only thing that came to mind.

'I've missed you.'

If it hadn't been for those three words...

Caitlin looked at the man sprawled in her bed with the stamp of lazy ownership embedded in the very core of his lean, elegant body. He was as addictive as the finest of Belgian chocolate and she couldn't peel her eyes away from his reflection in the mirror as she brushed her hair.

It was eight thirty. It was Sunday. They'd been talking about Alejandro and his rapid recovery. He had left the hospital a mere six weeks previously, but only now was he really fit to travel and he was packing up to return to London.

He was a changed man, light of heart and easy of spirit. Friends and family had been so supportive, he had repeatedly told Caitlin, in between preaching to her about the dangers of going out with his brother.

'Although,' he had mused only three days previously, 'he does seem to have changed. Very understanding about the whole work thing. I'm going to be heading up a team overseeing a new direction with the company. Boutique hotels. Three of them. Much more my thing than pretending to be interested in the financial side of things. He seems relaxed and I'm not the only one to have said that. He's been in touch with our parents several times since he went to London to take over, and off his own bat, which has always, it seems, been a rare occurrence. He's less stressed out. You've obviously removed a couple of his high-energy batteries when he wasn't looking.'

As a postscript, he had added, mischievously, 'At any rate, it's put Luisa fully in the picture. I had no idea she'd been that set on Dante.'

'Luisa's spending lots of time with your brother,' Caitlin said now, standing up and blushing because she recognised the brooding, sensual appreciation in his gaze as his eyes rested on her, naked and fresh from a shower.

'Poor Alejandro. The woman has always clung to our family like a limpet. Come to bed.'

'I know you said that that's because she has no family of her own.' Why was she worried about Luisa? Caitlin didn't know and her run-ins with her had been few, but she didn't trust the woman and her hands were tied when it came to saying anything to Alejandro because he never saw the bad in anyone. Besides, there was no way that she could set her sights on brother number two, bearing in mind that Alejandro had come clean about his sexuality! But the other woman's name had cropped up time and again, indicating a presence on the scene that felt vaguely threatening.

'Come to bed...' Dante repeated, and Caitlin smiled, their eyes still locking in the mirror on the wall.

Her breasts ached and her limbs felt languorous and there was a familiar ache between her thighs.

She'd never been so uninhibited. He did that to her. He'd shown up on her doorstep a month ago, had uttered those three words, and she'd been his. Her determination not to be swept away on a tide of pointless emotion had bitten the dust in record time. *He'd missed her.* There had been a naked honesty in that statement of fact and it had echoed her own feelings. She had opened the door to him and even as she was doing so, she had been helplessly aware that the common sense that had driven her departure a fortnight previously was going to be ditched.

'I have things to do.'

'With me.'

'I have a deadline to finish a layout on that shoot I did last week...'

She was smiling, though, and not moving as he eased himself off the bed, splendid in all his proud, masculine, impressive and very turned-on glory.

He absently held himself as he strolled towards her, then he was standing behind her, so much taller and broader, his bronzed skin such a striking contrast to her own smooth, milky pallor. Two naked lovers, looking at one another in the mirror, eyes tangling. There was something wildly erotic about the way they were standing, her back pressed against his chest. He reached to cover her breast with one hand

and she arched back, eyelids fluttering as he caressed it. Through half-closed eyes, she followed the motion of his fingers as they played with her pulsing nipple, teasing it, rubbing the stiffened peak. When he licked his finger and touched her again, she groaned and squirmed. He leant down to kiss her neck but he wouldn't let her turn around.

'I like you watching what I'm doing to you,' he murmured in a husky, shaky voice. 'Can you feel how hard I am for you right now?'

In response, Caitlin reached back to lightly touch him. She stroked the tip of his erection, a feathery caress, one she knew he liked. She felt him stiffen and smiled drowsily.

'You were saying something about work…' Dante breathed.

'I was…'

'Then I'd best not keep you and if we climb into bed, then you won't be getting much work done any time soon.'

Caitlin had to acknowledge that this was, indeed, very true. Dante never rushed things. When they lay in bed, he took his time. He touched her slowly, exploring every inch of her body until she was begging him for release. He was a man who could put his own desires on hold for as long as it took to satisfy hers. It showed a lack of selfishness when it came to making love and she had dimly registered, somewhere along the line, that underneath the sometimes ruthless and always sweepingly self-assured exterior was a guy who was, essentially, not driven at all by ego.

There was an overriding sense of fair play about him that was admirable. Both Dante and Alejandro had so many admirable qualities, in fact, that it was shocking that their relationship had disintegrated so much over the years, and she knew that one of the really great things to have emerged from the situation had been the slow meeting of ways between them, a gradual journey discovering themselves as brothers and appreciating that the bond that had been lost could be rebuilt with effort and goodwill.

She looked at Dante in the mirror, the incline of his dark head as he nuzzled her neck, and she was filled with a wave of such tenderness that she was, momentarily, disoriented and terrified.

'We'll just have to be quick,' he was saying, his voice muffled because he was talking against her neck.

As he said that, he slipped his finger against the wet crease between her legs, and that momentary jolt of *awareness*, a feeling that something inside her was changing somehow, was lost as pure sensation took over.

She clutched his wrists with her hands, then they fell slack to her sides for a second, before she balled her hands into tight fists, straining against the rhythm of his finger as he stroked, delving deeper with each stroke, building up a tempo that left her breathless.

Their reflection in the mirror was unfocused because her eyes were half closed. She was dimly aware of their bodies pressed tightly together, her body at the forefront, partially concealing his. One big hand rested on her breast, the other was moving between her legs. Their eyes collided and she licked her lips in a gesture that was unconsciously erotic.

He'd said quick. She was going to oblige because she could feel the rise of her orgasm, starting as a ripple then growing in intensity until it was taking over and she spasmed in a rush against his hand, crying out and arching back, her whole body stiffening as she came.

For a while, her mind was a complete blank, then gradually she came down from that peak and swivelled so that she was facing him. She touched his sides lightly, running her hands up and down and delighting in the feel of muscle and sinew. She stroked his inner thigh, then she knelt in front of him and teased him with her mouth and her tongue.

Dante curled his fingers into her hair.

She could turn him on like no one else on the planet, turn him on to the point where he lost the ability to think. He gave a guttural sound of satisfaction as she remorselessly pleasured him with her mouth and when he could hold out no longer, he came with a shudder that ripped through him, sending him rocking back on his feet.

And she still had work to do, she thought!

But he could do this to her, point her in a direction, knowing that she would follow because, with him, she was helpless.

Caitlin didn't get it because she had never been a helpless person. Even in the aftermath of her break-up with Jimmy, she had moved on, keeping herself to herself and picking up all the pieces without fuss. If London had overwhelmed her when she'd first arrived, then she had, likewise, taken it in her stride and faced down the unknown because what was the worst that could happen? She had her health.

But Dante...this man...

He made her feel helpless. She knew that she had ended up doing what she had told herself she would never do, had ended up caving in to her emotions and that cowardice had made her vulnerable. Very vulnerable.

A world imagined without him was no world at all.

She had gone and done what she had been cautioned against. She had fallen in love with him and as she dithered and wondered what to do about it, the days went by, each one making her more dependent than the one before.

Meanwhile, loose ends piled up around her. She was saving hard, steadfastly ignoring Dante's insistence that she move in with him, move in to the vast penthouse apartment in Mayfair that he had used as a base in the past whenever he'd happened to be in London. That final step, she knew, would be a huge mistake. At least her little one-bedroom flat was hers and he had given up trying to persuade her out of it. His solution was to avoid it at all costs because the area made him feel uncomfortable and, gradually, Caitlin had grown accustomed to a life largely led in his rarefied part of the world.

The money Alejandro had transferred was still sitting in her account, untouched.

He refused to give her the details of his bank account so that she could transfer it back to him.

He'd told her that it had been thanks to her that he had finally moved forward with his life and was no longer trapped in a cage of his own making.

He owed everything to her, he had confided the last time she had telephoned him and brought it up.

She would give him back the cash, she decided, just as soon as he was back in London, which would be in five days' time.

Face to face, he would have to cave because she would just refuse to leave him alone until he did.

Looking back on everything, she understood why she had agreed to the arrangement and yet, somehow, when she thought of that cash, she was overwhelmed with a feeling of guilt and unease.

She knew that she was enjoying life with a desperation that could only end in tears, so when, the day before Alejandro was due to arrive back in London, she glanced up from the kitchen table where she was meticulously looking at a series of photos she had taken two days previously, to see Dante framed in the doorway to the kitchen, she was almost resigned to the axe about to fall.

It was there in his expression. She realised that she had become accustomed to him strolling in to greet her with a smile that was part pleasure, part desire. Without even consciously thinking about it, she had been lulled into a state of security that had always been fragile at the very best. God, she was in *his* kitchen, as comfortable as though it were her own! She had fallen into the trap of thinking that she could tame a tiger.

Even in the depths of passion he had never, not once, offered anything other than what had been put on the table from the very start. Impermanence. Passing enjoyment. Lust.

His expression was cool. He stared at her until she fidgeted, angry with him for his silence and with herself for the fear that was filling up inside her.

'Too good to be true,' he rasped stonily, 'is what comes to mind when I look at you.'

He clenched his jaw and for a moment he was catapulted back to Luisa, her unexpected knock on his office door less than an hour and a half ago. He hadn't welcomed her in. In fact, he had risen to his feet to escort her out but as he had moved impatiently towards her, she had extended her hand with a piece of paper grasped in her fingers.

'Before you throw me out—' she had halted him in his tracks '—you need to have a look at this.'

'You need to leave my office, Luisa.' But his eyes had already been drawn to the single piece of paper and he had snatched it because it had seemed the fastest way of getting rid of the woman. He had listened to Caitlin's intermittent noises about Luisa and had played them down, omitting to tell her that he had fended off an unpleasant phone call from the other woman shortly after he had arrived in London. Why open a can of worms? The minute Luisa had accosted him in his office, he had assumed that she was going to pursue her plea to think about their long family connection and the value of resurrecting their defunct relationship.

This time, he'd thought, he wasn't going to bother with politeness.

He had half looked at that damning sheet of paper and then had looked more carefully.

Now, standing in his kitchen, he could still feel the cold fury that had swept through him when he had registered what was written.

But before the fury…

The devastation of realising that, once again, he had been sucked into a relationship with a woman who had not been what she had seemed.

Worse, he had realised, with shock, that there was something beyond devastation, beyond rage at his lack of judgement.

There had been the raw pain of knowing that what he'd felt for Caitlin had been far deeper than he could

possibly have imagined, and on the back of that pain
had come icy rage.

The self-discipline that was so much a part of
his personality had masked all emotion as he had
politely frozen Luisa out of the satisfaction of en-
gineering the outcome she had anticipated, but his
rage had not abated.

And now…standing here…

'Where did you get this?' Colour drained away
from her face and her hand was shaking.

If ever there was a picture of guilt, he thought
bitterly. What had he expected? Really? Some crazy
explanation that might make sense?

Unfortunately, he knew exactly what he had expected. He had expected her to be different. When
he looked back, he knew that he had thought her
different from the very first moment he had clashed
with her as she had skulked up the long avenue that
led to his mansion. She had intrigued him, and she
had continued to intrigue him, and when everything
had come out in the wash about his brother he had
done the unthinkable. He had dropped his guard and
given her the benefit of the doubt.

For the first time in his life he had begun to play
with the crazy notion of longevity.

He should have stuck to the brief and he was paying for straying from it now.

'Where?' she repeated. The beautiful lean lines of
his face were unforgiving and she could understand
why. She had come to know this man in many little

ways, and for him to have proof positive that there had been more to her relationship with Alejandro than an altruistic desire to help him in his hour of need by pretending to be his fiancée would signal the death knell to whatever he might have felt for her. Not love, no. But affection, yes, and certainly desire.

The email to the bank was brief, simply giving Alejandro's private banker instructions to transfer a hefty amount of money to her account.

'Does it matter?' Dante asked with glacial indifference.

Naturally it would have made zero difference if she had tried to blag her way out of this, but he was still enraged that she was making no effort to even try, and angry with himself for caring one way or the other.

The game was up and she was showing her true colours. No more eager desire to please.

'I don't suppose it does,' Caitlin said in a low voice. She couldn't meet his eyes. She couldn't bear the cold accusation there, the *disappointment.*

'Is that all you have to say?' Dante gritted. '*"I don't suppose it does"*? For the record, Luisa came by it and very thoughtfully decided to hand it over.'

'Of course she did,' Caitlin said wearily.

'Luisa may be many things but her faults have always been out in the open. She happened to be helping my brother pack his things and when he was out of the room, she accidentally refreshed his computer when she went to pick it up and curiosity got the better of her when your name popped up on the heading along with an account number. Quite a substantial sum of money, I must say. A good day at the office, wouldn't you agree?' He breathed in deeply and watched as colour suffused her. 'What were your plans for the money? Well-deserved spending spree? And did you decide that I might have been a more lucrative bet than my brother because if you managed to hook me, you might just have yourself a permanent passport to wealth instead of a one-off? Did you start as a fake fiancée only to imagine that you could become a real one but with the other heir to the throne?'

'How could you say that?' This time she *did* look at him, and with distress. 'Don't you know me at all?'

'It would seem not,' Dante grated harshly.

The truth was that he'd felt as though he *did* know her and even now, with the evidence of his own stupidity right in front of him, he *still* felt as if he did. It was an act of wilful self-delusion that enraged him further.

'Would you even make an effort to believe me if I told you that…' she sighed and blinked away a rush of miserable tears '…that it's not what you think, despite what it looks like?'

'It looks like you had a financial arrangement with my brother to cover your agreement to pose as his fiancée for the benefit of friends and family and to get our parents off his back on the business of marrying him off. How am I doing so far?'

Caitlin stared at him mutely.

'I'm gathering from your silence that I'm doing pretty good. Except you got here, and things didn't quite go according to plan. I should have paid a bit more attention to your striking lack of luggage when you arrived. I'm assuming the jaunt was supposed to be short-lived? A one-night charade then back to normal with a much-inflated bank account?'

'You're seeing it all in black and white…' But actually, every single word was spot-on and there was nothing she could do to defend herself. Her own sense of guilt would have stopped her anyway.

'No wonder you were so panicked at the thought of hanging around. Until, that is, you discovered that a little hanging around might work in your favour.'

'You know that's not true. You're making it out like I'm some sort of…of…*tramp*…some sort of… *sexual predator*…' She looked him squarely in the eye. 'You were my first, Dante.'

Dante had the grace to flush but then he aggressively told himself that that counted for very little when hard evidence of her mercenary nature was in front of him.

'Why are you still continuing with…' he waved his hand at the pile of photos spread across her side of the kitchen table '…*that*?' He vaulted forward, too restless to stay still any longer, and prowled the room before coming to stand in front of her, a towering and intimidating figure. 'And why are you still living in that dump? What was the money for, Caitlin? Debts?'

'Something like that.'

'What debts?' Dante didn't understand and he didn't like the feeling. 'Forget it,' he snapped, slashing the air with his hand in a gesture of conclusion. 'I'm going to go out for an hour. In that time, I want you to pack whatever things you might have here and leave. Put it this way, when I get back I don't want to find you still here.'

Dante was never going to listen to what she had to say, Caitlin realised. He had made his mind up. The only way he would ever have entertained hearing her out would have been if he had loved her, because if he had he would see what she saw, that it wasn't black and white but a thousand shades of grey, and he would have understood.

She was realising now what the fundamental difference between lust and love was.

Lust was essentially self-centred. It went so far when it came to seeing the bigger picture, to listening and forgiving, and no further.

Love was what bridged the gap, jumped over the chasm, having faith that you would reach the other side and being willing to take the risk.

She loved Dante and she knew that, had the shoe been on the other foot, she would have listened because she would have known, in her gut, that there was no way he could be the person circumstances were portraying him to be, that there would be another explanation, however things might look on the surface.

Well, there was no point hanging around and hoping for the impossible.

She nodded quietly. 'I'll be gone by the time you get back.'

CHAPTER TEN

IN THE EVENT it was two days before Dante returned to the penthouse apartment.

One hour? There was no way he intended to risk returning to find her still there, hunting around for the last of her things and, frankly, considering the fact that she had refused to move in with him, she had managed to find homes for a lot of her personal possessions. A couple of photography books here and there…spare bedroom slippers because she had to have something on her feet when she walked around…a selection of novels, all started and not one finished because she always lost interest somewhere between Chapter Three and Chapter Four…

He hadn't wanted to head back even after a day just in case she had forgotten something and had decided to return to collect it. He had forgotten to ask her to hand over the spare key he had insisted she have. She might have kept it. Who knew? She would leave it behind her in the apartment. He knew that without having to ask himself how.

So Dante had gone off grid for the first time in his

life, dumping London altogether and heading to the coast for a couple of days to clear his head.

She was gone. She'd pulled the wool over his eyes and she was gone. End of story.

He would pick up where he had left off because the world was full of beautiful women and he knew, without a trace of vanity, that he could have any of them.

Including Luisa, should he so choose, but the very thought of her made his teeth grind together. Like the messenger carrying a poisonous communication, she had been sliced out of his life for good, whatever the long-standing family connections. What she had done had been done with the worst of self-serving motives. He would wait until she tried to get in touch, which she inevitably would, to tell her exactly what he thought, but right now he just couldn't be bothered.

He couldn't be bothered with anyone or anything. He escaped London thinking that he would escape Caitlin. It had been a remarkable failure on that front.

Dante spent the first night drinking way too much at the Michelin-starred restaurant in the hotel where he had booked for the two nights.

Then he spent the second night wondering what the hell he was going to do because things seemed as clear as mud.

But by the time he began the journey back to London, clarity was imposing itself.

Without the benefit of distractions, he could think,

and in the confines of his Maserati, as he drove back
to London, he finally began to see what had been
lurking on the sidelines of his mind for so long now.
Like wisps of smoke, warning him of a conflagra-
tion. He should have paid attention.

The warning bells should have started sounding
the very second he'd decided to cross that ocean and
meet her again. Then he had entered a comfort zone
without even realising it. He had become accustomed
to the way she laughed and looked at him, to the
comfortable silences between them.

He hadn't been fazed by the sight of her tooth-
brush next to his or her photos spread across his
kitchen table, as they had been when he had con-
fronted her about that damned email.

Dante began joining all the dots on his way back
to London and by the time he hit the crowded outskirts of the city, he was frantic to do what he should
have done a long time ago. He had to be honest. He
had to stop pretending that he was an island.

He had to move on from hard and fast notions
that had dominated his life and kept his emotions
under lock and key.

But first and foremost, he had to convince her to
hear him out. He stopped at his apartment only to
dump his bag and have a rushed shower.

All evidence of her had been carefully removed.

The place was immaculate, wiped clean of her
presence. Not even the faintest of smells lingered.

That flowery, clean smell that followed her wherever she went? Gone.

He knew the way to her apartment like the back of his hand, even though he had, very quickly, refused to go there, preferring the comfort of his penthouse.

At a little after midday, there were signs of life, with kids out and about in front of the block of flats, aimlessly cycling around. He headed up to hers, nodding a greeting to some elderly lady with whom Caitlin had developed a firm friendship.

'She's not there.'

Dante stopped dead in his tracks. 'I have a key. I'll wait.'

Shared keys…something else that should have set those bells ringing in his head. Since when had he ever come close to handing a key to his place over to any woman, far less having a key for hers?

'You'll be waiting a long time, son.'

'Why?' Panic gripped him, like a vice.

'She's gone to her parents'. Told me to keep an eye on her place because she might be a while.'

'Her parents'?' He realised that, despite his knowing so much about her, she had singularly failed to talk to him about her parents. She had told him about her ex, about where she had grown up, had passed occasional remarks about her childhood, but her parents…? No, she hadn't mentioned them and suddenly that failing felt significant. 'Would you happen to have their address?'

She did. She handed it over. There were a lot of

questions, most of which Dante answered as honestly as he could and to the best of his ability, given that he was inept when it came to disclosing how he felt about anything with a complete stranger.

But he realised that he would, frankly, have done whatever it took to know how he could find the woman he had fallen hopelessly in love with.

He would climb a thousand mountains and walk a thousand miles, but on a more pressing level there was, he now realised, just one more thing he had to do first...

Caitlin heard the buzz of the doorbell. It was irritating, really, because this was the sixth night at her parents' house and the first evening she had had in on her own. The previous nights had been spent doing the rounds, as she had had to do the minute she'd appeared, unannounced, on her parents' doorstep.

It was a small village and people would have been offended if she hadn't immediately dropped by. Where her parents lived, being a recluse was practically a punishable offence, and it had been pretty reassuring visiting a couple of her parents' friends, knowing that they knew about the dire situation and were supportive.

The local vicar, another on the list of people she had seen and the first person who had shown up within hours of her arrival, was also fully in the know and very sympathetic.

They were all trying to keep spirits upbeat.

Everyone was rallying around.

Notwithstanding, that still left the matter of the finances that needed sorting out and this was her first evening in when she could really get down to seeing what was going on.

Her parents were out for the evening, dinner at friends'.

So the buzz of the doorbell, which she knew heralded another well-intentioned visitor, was…*irritating*.

She took her time getting to the door. She hoped that whoever was there might slink off, thinking that the house was empty.

But there was another buzz and so she pulled open the door and…

Déjà vu.

Hadn't she been here before? Staring at muscular legs encased in faded black jeans? At a body she had touched a million times? A face whose lines she knew from memory?

Hadn't this guy shown up, unannounced, on her doorstep once upon a time?

All those thoughts flashed through Caitlin's head in the seconds it took for her to register Dante's shocking appearance at the door.

'I know.' He tried a smile on for size. 'You're going to tell me that we've been down this road before.'

His voice was lazy and controlled but his heart wasn't. He was standing on the edge of a precipice, gazing down at a sheer drop and he wasn't sure whether there would be a safety net for when he took the plunge.

Rendered speechless, Caitlin could only gape.

'I went to your apartment.' Dante filled in the silence. He had to because he didn't want her to slam the door in his face. He could have inserted himself into the house, but that he didn't want to do because he was here with a begging bowl and he wasn't about to forget that. 'I met your neighbour. She told me where you were. She gave me your parents' address… so here I am.' He shuffled uncomfortably and flushed. Desperation bloomed. She wasn't saying a word and her expression told him nothing.

'Caitlin…'

'Stop right there!'

Why was he here? He had kicked her out of his life without giving her a chance to say her piece. He hadn't been interested then so…had he come bearing more tasty damning morsels? She didn't know and she didn't want to find out.

'You have *no right* to just show up at my parents' house! You should *never* have been given the address.'

'I've made mistakes…' He looked down, then raised his eyes to meet hers.

'Is that what you've come to tell me?'

'Please let me in.'

'I already did,' Caitlin said bitterly. 'I let you in and it was the biggest mistake I ever made.'

'Don't say that. I don't want to have this conversation out here, on the doorstep. I know your parents are probably in and… I am happy to talk to you with them present.'

'What?'

'What I have to say, I would be happy for them to hear.'

Caitlin hadn't been expecting that and she hesitated. If he was here about the wretched money, then she might as well get it over and done with. She pulled open the door with marked reluctance and stood back as he walked past her into the house.

He looked around and she saw what he did, but through his eyes. A small but tidy house. Her mother had always been house-proud, and her dad had never minded a bit of DIY, and the house reflected this. In her mind's eye, she saw his magnificent estate, the vast mansion shrouded in privacy, the acres of marble that told a tale of impossible riches, a penthouse with a priceless and exquisite Chagall painting hanging in the cloakroom, just the sort of casual afterthought only a billionaire could ever afford. Anger tasted like bile in her throat when she imagined him writing her off as a cheap, nasty gold-digger.

She walked towards the kitchen and was aware of him following in her wake.

'My parents are out at the moment,' she offered tersely, 'but they'll be back soon and I don't want you around when they get back. I don't want to have to explain…anything.'

'The last time I showed up unannounced,' Dante

said, declining the cup of coffee she offered although he knew he could do with a stiff drink in its place, 'I told you that I missed you.'

Caitlin blushed a furious red and waited in silence for him to get on with it. She'd been a sucker once and she wasn't about to repeat the exercise.

He was still standing but he sat down now and so did she, like two strangers facing one another in a boardroom, not quite sure how the meeting was going to go. Her spine was rigid and her fingers were curled over her knees in a defensive, vice-like grip.

'When I saw that email,' Dante plunged right in, still very much conscious of the fact that he could be chucked out at any given moment and he wouldn't blame her, 'I... I felt like the bottom of my world had dropped out. I couldn't have been more shocked and I reacted in just the way I was programmed to react.' He held up one hand because he could see that she was on the point of interrupting and he just needed to carry on saying what he had to say, had to gather momentum and run. It was the only way he was going to be able to hurl himself off the edge of that damned precipice.

Caitlin was riveted. He shouldn't be here. She shouldn't be listening to him. But there was a gut-wrenching, despairing honesty about him that held her rapt.

'I'd been let down once and, after that, I built a wall around myself. There was no way that I was ever going to be let down again. Then I got that email and read it and realised that I'd done the unthinkable. I had dropped all my defences. It was the only thing that could account for the sickening feeling in the pit of my stomach, the feeling that my world had stopped turning.' He breathed in deeply and realised his heart was racing. 'You don't believe me?'

'You've never said anything like this before.'

'I didn't…know how.'

'I'm not drifting back into some sort of relationship with you because you still want me in your bed.'

'When I said that I missed you, I should have said the bits I miss most aren't the ones where you occupy my bed. Not that I don't miss those.'

'I don't know what you're trying to tell me.'

'I'm trying to tell you that I don't care. I don't care about whatever financial arrangement you had with my brother. I don't care whether you needed the money to cover a lifestyle of fast cars and gambling dens.'

Caitlin raised both eyebrows. She was still clutching her knees, but the white-knuckle ride was abating and something inside her was melting.

'You didn't even hear me out,' she said painfully. 'You just went ahead and assumed the worst.'

'I did and I will regret that for the rest of my life.'

'You searched me out once, Dante, because you felt that what we had should have carried on. I'm not that same person any longer.' She really wasn't, she thought. She was way too involved to risk having her heart broken all over again.

'I don't expect you to carry on with what we had,' Dante told her seriously. 'It wouldn't be what I wanted. I don't want a fling with you, *querida*. I want the rest of my life with you.'

Caitlin blinked and gaped.

'You're kidding…'

Dante reached into his pocket. The black box had been burning a hole there since he had entered her house. That thing he'd had to do, the final step he'd had to take.

The box sat in the palm of his hand, then he opened it, his dark eyes firmly pinned to her face, registering her tremulous disbelief, then the dawning smile that told him that everything was going to be just fine.

'Far from it. I'm deadly serious. I love you and I can't envisage a life without you in it. I want you to wear this ring and then I want you to wear my wedding ring next to it.'

Caitlin stared then she smiled and tentatively reached out to touch the ring with one finger. It was the most beautiful thing she had ever seen, a solitaire diamond glittering in its bed of white gold, and on the band were tiny diamonds, like perfect tiny stars paying homage to that single, glittering and much bigger one that nestled in the centre.

'Am I dreaming?' she murmured to herself. She raised her eyes, barely able to breathe.

'You're not dreaming.' He took a chance and slipped the ring onto her finger and then stared in silence because this was the biggest thing he had ever done in his life before. It literally rendered him speechless. He gently stroked her finger before continuing gravely, 'I had a few days away from everything after you left and I came to my senses. It took me a while. But how could I recognise the symptoms of something I'd never felt before?'

'You want to spend the rest of your life with me?' She couldn't stop staring at the ring, now on her finger, the perfect fit.

'Why do you think I told you that I would have this conversation in front of your parents? I want to marry you, Caitlin Walsh, so will you say yes?'

'Just try and stop me.' She breathed unsteadily, then went over to him and curled herself onto his lap, her arms flung round his neck, loving the tightness of his embrace.

'The money thing...' She pulled back and looked at him and sighed.

He reached to shush her but she held his finger in her hand and squeezed it.

Then she stood up and pulled a chair right up next to his so that her legs were pressed between his and she could rest her hands on his thighs. The gleaming diamond, so much a tangible statement of intent, so much *Dante*, who was a man of such intent, gave her the strength to come clean and broach the topic that had severed their relationship.

'Where to start? I knew that Alejandro was terrified about coming out. I think he felt that he had gone as far as he could resisting his parents' efforts to marry him off and, in his desperation, he came up with the idea of me posing as his fiancée, basically to bide time until…until you decided to settle down, which would take the heat off him. It was a crazy idea, really, and I didn't want to go along with it but I felt sorry for him. He said that it would be a business deal and I refused.'

She felt tears trying to leak out of the corners of her eyes as she thought back to the train of events that had led to her changing her mind.

'I kept refusing and then two things happened in very quick succession. My parents ran into some terrible financial debt. My dad had been scammed and he'd been keeping it quiet. I found out and basically…he'd been conned out of all his savings. I won't go into the details, but it was very clever. He was mortified. His pension isn't huge, and those savings were going to be the foundation for their old age. Of course, I told them that I would help, but shortly after my mother had a heart attack. Stress induced, the doctor said.' She sighed. 'And there was Alejandro, with that plan still at the back of his mind. I caved in. I took him up on his offer. So you see, there were debts but not mine and not of my making.' She paused. 'Only thing was I hadn't banked on the guilt. I couldn't take the money in the end. Maybe if it had all stayed as a business arrangement, but then things happened and I got involved with you… The money is untouched and I intend to force it back to

Alejandro as soon as he gets to London. He refuses to let me have his account details so I might just have to show up with a few sacks of coins and bills.' She smiled. 'I don't blame you for suspecting the worst.'

'You should blame me for everything,' Dante told her gravely. 'Most of all for being a fool and almost letting you go. Trust me, I intend to spend the rest of my life making you happy.' He leant forward and drew her towards him and kissed her.

It felt as if he was coming home. It was just where he wanted to be.

There was a lavish wedding in Spain. Tradition, Dante had told her wryly, was tradition and his parents were finally getting the wedding they had wanted for a while. Both sets of parents hit it off and there was so much parental involvement on both sides that Caitlin wasn't quite sure just how vital her contributions were.

But it all went off without a hitch. The dress was spectacular, as was the awesome cathedral. Her heart fluttered and her mouth ran dry the minute her eyes found Dante waiting for her with his brother to his right, the very proud ring bearer.

Then, a mere handful of days later, there was a far smaller do close to her parents' home, where family and friends celebrated the union over a home-cooked meal prepared by the caterer at the one and only hotel in the village.

The honeymoon was wonderful. Two weeks in

the Maldives, where all those problems that had afflicted her once upon a time seemed very long ago.

But then, she was living a new life now, with the man she loved.

That very man was right at this moment pouring her a glass of wine while she relaxed on the sofa, a lovely vantage point from which she could appreciate him.

The honeymoon had come and gone. Reality of life with Dante was even sweeter than she could possibly have imagined.

'We need to sort out where we're going to live.' He handed her the glass and Caitlin dutifully rested it on the low coffee table next to her.

'Now that my brother is jet-setting in his new role, I think London will be my base. Naturally we can return to Madrid whenever we wish, but I feel that this would be more suitable for us, as a couple.'

Caitlin nodded and tried to imagine bringing up a family in a penthouse. Glass and toddlers were not a happy mix. Should she mention that now?

'And not here.' He grinned.

'Since when did you become a mind reader?'

'It's called being in love.'

She was wearing some comfy track pants and a baggy top and when she shuffled along the sofa to snuggle against him, the warmth of her little body suffused him with the sort of deep contentment he had never envisaged for himself.

'Where were you thinking?' she asked, inclining her head so that their eyes met.

'To be decided. We can discuss where but I'm thinking within commuting distance from London but far out enough to be surrounded by some open land. And, of course, more in the direction of your parents.'

'That's a good idea,' Caitlin murmured, 'because we're going to need a bit of space and a bit of land and less sharp corners and glass surfaces.'

'We are?' Dante stilled, his sharp eyes noticing that the wine, her favourite brand, was untouched.

'I only found out this morning and I wanted to surprise you, my darling…'

'You've succeeded.' He angled her so that he could kiss her and kiss her he did. Then he looked at her and stroked her face with such tenderness that her heart expanded until it wanted to burst.

'A baby on the way.' He couldn't stop grinning. 'I love you, my darling. You make my life complete and a baby to come? It couldn't get any better…'

* * * * *

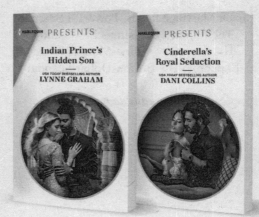

#3853 THEIR IMPOSSIBLE DESERT MATCH
by Clare Connelly
A chance encounter between Princess Johara and a mystery lover was the perfect night. Until she discovers the man was her family's bitter enemy! Now Johara must travel to Sheikh Amir's desert palace to broker peace...and try to resist their forbidden temptation!

#3854 STEALING THE PROMISED PRINCESS
The Kings of California
by Millie Adams
Prince Javier de la Cruz's goal was simple. Tell heiress Violet King she's promised in marriage to his brother. His first problem? She refuses. His second problem? Their instant, unwelcome and completely forbidden chemistry!

#3855 HOUSEKEEPER IN THE HEADLINES
by Chantelle Shaw
Betsy Miller was ready to raise her son alone after tennis legend Carlos Segarra dismissed their night of passion. Now that the headlines have exposed their child, Carlos is back and everyone's waiting to see what he'll do next...

#3856 ONE SCANDALOUS CHRISTMAS EVE
The Acostas!
by Susan Stephens
Smoldering Dante Acosta has got to be physiotherapist Jess's sexiest client yet. Even injured, the playboy polo champion exudes a raw power that makes Jess giddy...but can she depend on him fighting for their chemistry this Christmas?

YOU CAN FIND MORE INFORMATION ON UPCOMING HARLEQUIN TITLES, FREE EXCERPTS AND MORE AT HARLEQUIN.COM.

HPCNMRB0920

Get 4 FREE REWARDS!

We'll send you 2 FREE Books plus 2 FREE Mystery Gifts.

PRESENTS

Cinderella in the Sicilian's World
USA TODAY BESTSELLING AUTHOR
SHARON KENDRICK

PRESENTS

Proof of Their Forbidden Night
USA TODAY BESTSELLING AUTHOR
CHANTELLE SHAW

Harlequin Presents books feature the glamorous lives of royals and billionaires in a world of exotic locations, where passion knows no bounds.

FREE Value Over **$20**

Love Harlequin romance?

DISCOVER.

Be the first to find out about promotions,
news and exclusive content!

 Facebook.com/HarlequinBooks

Twitter.com/HarlequinBooks

Instagram.com/HarlequinBooks

Pinterest.com/HarlequinBooks

ReaderService.com

EXPLORE.

Sign up for the Harlequin e-newsletter and
download a free book from any series at
TryHarlequin.com

CONNECT.

Join our Harlequin community to
share your thoughts and connect
with other romance readers!
Facebook.com/groups/HarlequinConnection